John Henry Parker

Historical Photographs

a systematic catalogue of Mr. Parker's collection of photographs

illustrative of the history of Rome - and of architecture, sculpture, and

drawing in Rome

John Henry Parker

Historical Photographs
a systematic catalogue of Mr. Parker's collection of photographs illustrative of the history of Rome - and of architecture, sculpture, and drawing in Rome

ISBN/EAN: 9783337361198

Printed in Europe, USA, Canada, Australia, Japan

Cover: Foto ©Andreas Hilbeck / pixelio.de

More available books at **www.hansebooks.com**

HISTORICAL PHOTOGRAPHS.

A

SYSTEMATIC CATALOGUE

OF

MR. PARKER'S COLLECTION OF PHOTOGRAPHS

ILLUSTRATIVE OF THE

HISTORY OF ROME,

AND OF ARCHITECTURE, SCULPTURE, AND DRAWING IN ROME,

ARRANGED ACCORDING TO SUBJECTS.

PART I.

I. PRIMITIVE FORTIFICATIONS.
II. WALLS AND GATES OF ROME.
III. HISTORICAL CONSTRUCTION OF WALLS.
IV. THE AQUEDUCTS.
V. THE EGYPTIAN OBELISKS.

SOLD BY

WILLIAM SPOONER,

379, STRAND, LONDON.

1872.

PRIMITIVE FORTIFICATIONS.

PREFACE.

THE numerous excavations carried on in Rome during the last few years have thrown a new light on many obscure subjects, and not least, on the ancient earthworks, on which, and within which, the City of Rome was made. They have also shewn that the walls which formed part of these Fortifications were built of great blocks of tufa. Several things, which at first seemed bold and hazardous conjectures only, have eventually become matter of strict demonstration. It is now certain that these great blocks of stone were each of a ton weight (or each a load for a cart, as Dionysius says), and have in many cases been left in their original places, used as foundations for later buildings. Even when these later buildings have subsequently been rebuilt *from the foundations*, those foundations themselves have been left as they were, as there could not be better foundations to build upon.

These ancient walls now brought to light, could not have been visible in the Augustan age, nor could have been seen by Varro, or Cicero, or Livy, or Dionysius: it is therefore impossible that any of those authors could have written their works to fit these walls, which they could not have seen; hence when we find that the architectural character and the construction of these walls agree with their writings in the succession attributed to them, this fact goes far to demonstrate the substantial truth of the ancient history of Rome, legendary or traditional, as it may be,—but which has been handed down from father to son orally for many generations before it was committed to writing as history. That this history was fully believed by the writers of the Augustan age, is evident from the writings themselves, and from many inscriptions. The fragment of the beginning of a set of Fasti, of the time of Augustus, engraved on a marble tablet, dug up in the Forum in 1872, begins with "Romulus, the son of Mars." Of course, the mixture of the supernatural, and the mention of the gods, are only marks of the credulity of the people, and all historians have to separate the marvellous and the supernatural from the reality of history. In the celebrated inscription called *Monumentum Ancyrinum*, in which Augustus records the buildings he had erected, he says that he *made the Lupercal*, that is, he built a hall or chamber against the mouth of a cave, which he believed to have been a wolf's cave, under the north-west corner of the Palatine Hill. Such a cave still remains, with a fine stream of water gushing out into it, and with ruins of vaulted chambers of the time of Augustus in front of it.

Again, on the top of the Palatine, nearly over this cave, we have a wall of the earliest character of any wall in Rome, a continuation of which can be traced by portions of it still remaining and now made visible, on three sides of an oblong space at the north end of the hill. The earliest part is immediately opposite to the Hill of Saturn, occupied by the Sabines before the arrival of the Romans. There is also a wide and deep trench or foss across the hill on the southern side of this oblong space, and on both sides of the trench or valley there are remains of very early tufa walls; on the north side also, the part nearest to the enemies' quarter, are the lower parts of towers begun and left unfinished, and then used as foundations for later buildings.

On the Hill of Saturn are considerable remains of the great public building originally called the Capitolium, erected when it was agreed to make that hill the Capitol of the new city, consisting then of the two hills only. There are also considerable remains of the wall that enclosed these two hills, which is mentioned incidentally only by Dionysius; but this sort of incidental notice is more valuable even than a direct statement of the fact would be : he takes it for granted, as a thing that every body knows, that the temple of Castor and Pollux was built at the north-east corner of the Palatine Hill, "when the two hills were enclosed in one wall." The walls of that period, which we find to have been fifty or sixty feet high, and twelve feet thick, are not easily obliterated; but they are often misunderstood, and they have been so in this instance. Of this wall of the second City of Rome, the junction with the eastern cliff of the Hill of Saturn was brought to light in 1872, under a house in the Via di Marforio. This wall was one of enclosure for municipal purposes, the boundary of the new City, but not much intended as a fortification. An account of it is given in an Appendix to our third chapter on the " Historical Construction of Walls."

The other hills were fortified when they were first inhabited each as a separate fortress; but they were not included in the boundary of the City until the time of Servius Tullius. Each of these separate fortresses can be traced by existing remains of tufa walls of that early period. On the Aventine, where the Latins were settled after the conquest of their principal city of Alba Longa, these remains are very important and interesting, as we can there see more clearly than anywhere else the plan of these old fortifications (in the garden or vineyard of Prince Torlonia, near S. Prisca). We there see that the cliff has been scarped to the depth of fifty or sixty feet, and a terrace made on a ledge in the rock at the foot of this escarpment; and on this ledge we see further that the wall stands: that this wall is built in part of the great blocks of tufa, cut away from the surface of the cliff in the process of scarping it, and that other parts of similar blocks of a slightly different colour have been brought from a quarry in the same hill, very near to the spot; stones of a ton weight each are not easily brought from a distance. We notice that the wall, in its original state, was twelve feet thick, formed entirely of these large blocks, and that, in another part, it has been altered to introduce small arches, perhaps for catapults; that in this part the back of the wall is a mass of concrete faced only with the great blocks of tufa, and that the arches have been made in this outer facing, but these are evidently introduced at a subsequent period, though still an early one. We observe also that at the foot of this great wall was a trench, afterwards filled up, and deep pits made in it in the time of Trajan, connected with the *thermæ* of his cousin Sura.

This fortress is at the north-west angle of a gorge in the hill, at the narrow end of which was a gate, where four roads meet. On the opposite, or south angle of this gorge, are remains of another ancient fort, of which we have only the concrete mass of the wall; but at the foot of it we found, by excavations made in 1871, remains of the facing of large blocks of tufa, as on the other side. This second fort is under S. Sabba, on the Pseudo-Aventine, and that part of the hill appears to have been the arx or citadel of the Aventine when it was a separate fortress. The tufa wall remains at the other end of it under S. Balbina, still visible on the eastern side, as it was also on the northern side (when a photograph was obtained of it in 1868), before Signor Rosa had buried it in the earth that he brought from the Palatine and threw there. The church and monastery of S. Balbina is on the site of another ancient fort, of which the tufa walls could be seen on three sides of it, on the east and the north, as mentioned, and on the west also, where it has been excavated; on the south side, the trench has been filled up.

This ancient fort (now S. Balbina) is opposite to another on the Cœlian, in which the Villa Mattei or Cœlimontana has been built. These two ancient forts were used by Servius Tullius to protect the Porta Capena in his short *agger* across the valley, from the cliff of the Aventine to that of the Cœlian. The fort at the north-east corner of the Cœlian protected two other gates at the inner ends of other gorges, one in the southern cliff, now the entrance to the Piazza della Navicella from the Porta Metronia ; the other in the western cliff, going up nearly to the arch of Dolabella. That arch was the entrance into that part of the hill which was afterwards called the Claudium, made in another ancient fort on the south-western angle of the Cœlian, extending nearly to the site of the Colosseum. The scarped cliffs are very distinct on three sides. The Clivus Scauri passes between these two ancient forts on the western side of the hill. Between the Claudium and the other part of the Cœlian is another gorge, and the narrow end of this nearly meets that before-mentioned, near the arch of Dolabella. It would appear that the western end of the Cœlian, almost detached from the hill, was the arx or citadel of that hill as a separate fortress. On the north side of the hill, the church and monastery of the Santi Quattro Coronati stands, evidently in another ancient fort, with the cliff visible on three sides of it, and a trench on the south, cutting it off from the rest of the hill. This protected another gate, where the church of S. Clement now stands. Between the east end of the Cœlian and the Lateran fortress is another wide and deep foss, partly natural and partly cut, with walls against the cliffs on both sides, and tombs on both sides also, shewing that it was outside of the City. The Lateran has been probably made in the Cœliolum. The church of S. Clement, which stands upon another of these short *aggeres*, connected the Cœlian fortress and the Esquiline fortified hill ; the southern and eastern cliffs of that hill carry on the line to the junction with the great *agger* on the eastern side of Rome.

There are remains of the ancient fortifications of the Viminal on the cliff opposite to S. Vitale, and of the Quirinal in the Colonna Gardens, and in part of the gardens of Sallust (now those of Spithoever). The arx of the Esquiline was probably where the church of S. Pietro in Vincoli now stands, where the cliffs and the trenches are very visible ; that of the Viminal was probably where the ruins of towers were excavated in 1871, as mentioned ; that of the Quirinal was probably where the great palace is now situated.

All these separate fortresses were, of course, merged in the city of Servius Tullius. This third City of Rome was made by uniting the seven hills in one enclosure, making use of the previous ancient fortifications of separate villages, uniting them by *aggeres*, or banks of earth, faced with walls having deep and wide trenches in front of them, across the valley from the scarped cliffs of one hill to those of another, and by making the great *agger* of Servius Tullius on the high table-land on the eastern side of Rome. Of this there are considerable remains, long seen and acknowledged as such by all who have paid attention to the subject.

This third City was seven miles round; but nearly all fortifications require an outer wall of enclosure, called the "wall of *enceinte*," and the Tarquins endeavoured to supply this by another great bank and foss of far greater extent, making the circuit thirteen miles. The labour required for these great earthworks must have been enormous, and could only have been made by the whole population of the city being employed upon them for years. This could only have been done under a despotic government; but the people had not the same foresight as their rulers, and they at last rebelled against all this labour, of which they did not see the necessity. The rebellion under Brutus was successful, and the Republic was established, as we know. The great *mœnia*, or the outer line of defence, were left unfinished at both ends; nor was there any outer wall to the Aventine until the time of Claudius, and in the break between the Prætorian Camp and the Pincian Hill the outer earthworks were never erected. This was the weak part of the defences of Rome, and at this point it was repeatedly attacked and taken. Indeed, from that time there was an end to all great public works, until the time of Sylla the dictator.

To understand properly the ancient fortifications of Rome, where they are so much concealed by later work, it is necessary to look at those of other cities of the same early period, such as Fiesole, Volterra, and other Etruscan cities to the north; Tusculum, Alba Longa, and Gabii, on the eastern side. These have, we find, fortifications of precisely the same character, and far more perfect, though varying in details, according to their respective situations. Alba Longa is especially important, as being the reputed city from · which the first Romans emigrated; and Gabii, as having been another colony from Alba Longa. This town is built on precisely the same plan,—a single long street on the edge of a lake.

PRIMITIVE FORTIFICATIONS OF ROME.

[The numbers refer to Mr. Parker's Catalogue.]

Those marked with * are from drawings, valuable for historical purposes,
but not as photographs.

FIRST PERIOD, A.U.C. 1 to 30 (?),
  B.C. 753—720 (?).

THE PALATINE HILL.

Plan and Sections of that Hill.
  95*, 96*, 97*

Walls—General View of the north-west
corner of the Hill, shewing the tufa
Wall of Romulus (?) against the upper
cliff, with walls of the Republic and
of the Empire built up against it and
upon it.   106

—— View of a portion of the tufa Wall
separately, shewing the construction
at the *north-west* corner.   105, 779

—— Another part of the same Wall,
with Guard Chambers of a Palace of
the Cæsars, and stairs built against it.
                                    114

—— Remains of one of the unfinished
Towers of Romulus (?) on the terrace
at the north end.   1452

—— Remains of another of the unfinished Towers at the north end,
shewing portions of the two side walls
of tufa, with concrete wall of the Republic, and brickwork of the Empire
built upon them.   1453

—— Portion of another tufa Wall at
the *south-west* corner of the Arx or
Citadel of Romulus (?) (*Roma Quadrata*), on the *northern* side of his
great foss across the middle of the
Palatine Hill.   2235

—— Another portion of the same Wall,
afterwards used as the *podium* or basement of a temple; it stands upon the
tufa rock at the edge of the foss on
the northern side of it.   2232

Walls—Fragment of the tufa Wall on
the *southern* side of the foss, afterwards
used to support the side of a sloping
paved road of the time of the early
Empire; this wall is much decayed.
                                    2295

—— View of the south-east angle of
the Hill near the Colosseum, shewing the Scarped Cliff, with a Wall of
the Cæsars built up against it.   117

WALLS OF THE SAME PERIOD, FOR
  COMPARISON.

Tusculum — The Acropolis, Scarped
Cliffs and Gate. 1897, 1898, 1899, 1900

Alba Longa—Scarped Cliff with Wall.
                                    1939*

—— Cave Reservoir of Water, under
the Arx, with peculiar wells of conical
shape.   1940*

—— Similar Reservoir on the Palatine.   366*

Gabii—Scarped Cliffs with Wall, and
with the Modern Village, shewing
the character of the Primitive habita-
tions.   1582

Volterra—Etruscan Walls (under Santa
Chiara).   2394, 2395

SECOND PERIOD, A.U.C. 30—60 (?).

WALL ENCLOSING THE PALATINE AND
THE HILL OF SATURN IN ONE CITY.
(Dionysius, lib. i. c. 66.)

Plan and Sections of the Hill of Saturn,
afterwards the Capitol.   119*

View of the Tarpeian Rock.   120

Plan—Shewing the site of remains of
the wall extending from the north-
east corner of the Hill of Saturn (*then*

made the Capitol), part of it used to enclose the Forum of Augustus. 2962*

Excavations in the Via di Marforio, 1872, at the point of junction of the wall with the rock of the hill of Saturn. 2963*

Tufa Wall of the Kings on the Eastern side of the Forum of Augustus. 881

—— Section of the same Wall (now behind the houses), 50 ft. high and 12 ft. thick, with another Wall, a third of the height and thickness, inserted in it at a right angle. The latter wall is of travertine, and was the partition between the Forum of Augustus and the Forum Transitorium of Nerva. 844

Tufa Wall on the south side of the Forum Transitorium, behind the Marble Columns of the Temple of Pallas, which are built up against it, (this wall continues under the houses as far as the Tor de' Conti). 847

Tufa Wall on the west side of the Palatine, at a low level (now in a garden behind the houses). 98, 667*

Walls of Towers (now under the church of S. Anastasia), at the same low level (miscalled the Pulvinar of the Circus Maximus).
748 from nature, 100*, 102*

Tufa Wall on the bank of the Tiber, called the Pulchrum Littus.
159, 157*, 1171

THE AVENTINE HILL.

Scarped Cliffs—1. On the western side, with early wall (and the palace of the Savelli built upon it). 134

—— 2. At Western corner, supported by tufa wall. 139

—— 3. (Under S. Balbina) on the southern part, with tufa wall built against it (now concealed). 144, 802

Wall of the Latins (?) (near S. Prisca), with an arch inserted in the time of Camillus (?). 141, 749, 790

Ancient Fort under S. Sabba. 143

THE CŒLIAN OR CÆLIAN HILL.

Plan and Sections, by Ernest di Mauro. 2964*

Scarped Cliffs, north-east angle of the Arx of the Cœlian fortress, afterwards the Claudium, near the Colosseum. 123

Scarped Cliffs at the southern angle of the Arx, the Promontory under the Villa Mattei. 124

—— North-east Promontory, under the Monastery of the IV. Santi Coronati. 133

QUIRINAL, VIMINAL, AND ESQUILINE.

VIMINAL—Plan. 149*

—— Section. 148*

—— Tufa Wall against the Western Cliff of the Arx (opposite to S. Vitale). 150

ESQUILINE — Fort at the south-east angle, an arcade of the Early Empire built against a tufa wall. 147

QUIRINAL—Tufa Wall against the Cliff in the Colonna Gardens. 2113

THE GREAT AGGER OF SERVIUS TULLIUS.

Plan of the Horn-work at the northeast corner, afterwards in the Garden of Sallust. 842*

Ancient Cliff at the west end of the Horn-work. 154

Tufa Wall against this Cliff, at the west end. 1024

Arcade built against the north end. 153

Plan and Section of part of the Agger (near the Railway Station in 1868). 885*

West or Inner side of the Agger. 152

Section of the Agger and Wall. 151

THE SMALLER AGGERES OF SERVIUS TULLIUS.

1. From the southern cliff of the Esquiline to the northern cliff of the Cœlian (passing under the altar of the church of S. Clement), Wall in that part. 1263

2. From the south-west cliff of the Cœlian to the north-east cliff of the Aventine, (in this short *agger* the

Porta Capena was under the cliff of the Cœlian, and the Piscina Publica under that of the Aventine). Plan and Section of that valley, 632*. Interior of a tower of the Porta Capena, with the Aqua Marcia carried through it (and upon the arch of the gate). 710*

Views in the Pits dug in 1869 on the line of this *agger*, with remains of the Aqueducts upon it. 1164, 1165, 1166, 1244, 2221, 2222 Plans and Sections of this short *agger*. 1138*, 1139*, 1140*, 1141*, 1142*

There are remains of another short *agger* between the southern part of the Aventine (called the Pseudo-Aventine) and the northern part of that hill, which extends to the Tiber; and the cliffs of that hill, with the wall upon them (Nos. 140, 141, 790), forming part of the defence of the third City, or the City of Servius Tullius, on that side as far as the hill extended. The great tufa wall on the bank of the Tiber, called the Pulchrum Littus, was then the defence as far as the island. Another tufa wall, with a great foss in front of it, was then carried across from the bridge to the western side of the Hill of Saturn, afterwards the Capitol, the northern side of which was part of the defences of the second City. This foss can be traced through the Ghetto and the fish-market, and part of the tufa wall on the bank of it remains under the Church of S. Angelo in Pescheria.

WALLS AND GATES OF ROME.

PREFACE.

THE Walls and Gates of Rome are always considered as among the most interesting remains of antiquity that have been preserved to our time. Notwithstanding the numerous vicissitudes through which they have passed during so many centuries,—the sieges they have sustained,—the demolition ordered by the Goths in the fifth century, and begun, but only very partially carried out,—and the numerous repairs by successive Popes, each in the bad style of his period, together with the recent so-called *restorations*,—we still have many parts remaining of the time of the early empire, including several miles of the great wall of Aurelian, of the third century, and the gateway fortresses added by Stilicho, under Honorius, and repaired by Theodoric after the lapse of another century and the damages done by the Goths.

We have also some of the gateways of an earlier period (built upon the old earthworks), from the first century downwards, and other buildings which, standing on that outer bank, were incorporated in the great wall of Aurelian, on the extension of the boundary of the City beyond the inner works of Servius Tullius, to which it had been limited for several centuries. The Prætorian Camp and the Sessorium are the two most important ancient works included in this wall; but there are others also :—the Lateran Palace, with its gate; the Aqueducts for the space of a mile, from the Palace gardens of the Sessorium, where the water entered Rome, to the Prætorian Camp, passing over the two great eastern gates,—first, the Porta Maggiore, sometimes called the Porta Sessoriana, as well as Præ- nestina by those going to Præneste, Labicana by those going to Labicum, and Esquilina by those entering Rome through this gate into the Exquiliæ, long the public burial ground, and thence onwards to the Esquiline Hill. Near the Porta di S. Lorenzo is the outer wall of a fine reservoir of the second century, made for the Aqua Tepula, as rebuilt by Trajan : the remarkable feature in this wall is the series of marble corbels still remaining intact, which have car- ried a *hourd* (or wooden balcony). The *specus* or conduit of the Tepula, with its triangular head, is visible at an angle in the wall, where it entered into this great reservoir.

The Porta di S. Lorenzo was one of the gates leading to Tibur, or Tivoli, and was called the Porta Tiburtina by persons going there; but it was also called Porta Viminalis by persons entering Rome, and going through this gate to the Viminal Hill, as we are told by Frontinus, writing in the first century. The inscription of the time of Augustus, remaining on the face of the conduit over that gate, identifies it as the gate intended by him. That now called the Porta Chiusa, or the closed gate, at the south-western corner of the Prætorian Camp, was so called because people could not agree in the name of it when the gates were named in modern times. The exterior of this gateway is of the time of Honorius, but the interior is much earlier. There is no doubt that one of the roads to Tivoli went through this gate, and it was the most direct line; the old road, called Via Cupa, is very near to this at the further corner of the Prætorian Camp; it is a very ancient way, cut out of the solid rock of tufa for about half-a-mile; but from its depth and narrowness it was not convenient for carriages, and a new one was made from the Porta di S. Lorenzo to the church of the same name, upon a bank made across the great ancient foss of the City. This can still be seen to be the case from the vineyards, but the walls on each side conceal the fact from persons going along it; the old and the new roads met at the church. The proper name for the Porta Chiusa must be Porta Tiburtina, and the other gate is properly called after S. Lorenzo, as leading direct to that great church and burial-ground.

Near the Porta di S. Lorenzo, and close to the great reservoir of the Tepula before mentioned, is a square gate in the wall long closed; it was probably there before the time of Aurelian, and was closed at the time that wall was built. The old road from Præneste is believed to have passed through that gate, as it runs in a straight line towards it as far as the edge of the great external foss; but the part nearest Rome is closed for about two miles, and is accessible on foot or on horseback only. Another ancient gate, the Porta Ardeatina, leading to Ardea, was probably closed at the same time; the construction of its arch and piers is clearly of the time of Nero, the best period of brickwork; and the old way from that gate for half-a-mile out of Rome can be traced in the vineyards as far as the chapel called "Domine quo vadis," and the tomb of Priscilla opposite to it, with a round tower of the Medieval period built upon it. This is just the corner of the Via Ardeatina, at its junction with the Via Appia, and it is evident that the Via Ardeatina is older than the Via Appia, as the latter is made to deviate to the east, to allow space for the tombs on each side.

The usual manner of seeing the walls and gates is to take a drive along the outside of the walls on the eastern side of Rome, from the Porta del Popolo near the Tiber on the north, to the Porta di S. Paolo and Monte Testaccio near the Tiber again on the south, and this is a most interesting drive (or walk, for good walkers). This is the line described in the fourth section of this chapter, the description of the circuit of the walls, in which we have followed the Itinerary of Einsiedlen *. We have endeavoured to shew what still remains of the objects described in that minute account of the ninth century. The writer begins with a part of the wall along the bank of the Tiber on the west side of Rome, which is now either entirely destroyed, or what does remain is no longer visible, owing to the space being occupied by modern Rome, but when the water is low in the river the lower part of several towers can be seen. He also crosses the Tiber and gives an account of the wall in the Trastevere on the Janiculum, but not of the Leonine City, as he wrote before the time of Pope Leo, who founded it. He does, however, include the Hadrianum, the fortress to defend the gate of S. Peter, now the castle of S. Angelo. It is probable that the Mausoleum of Hadrian was always intended to be the centre of a great fortress, to defend a weak side of Rome, as, near this bend of the river there is a ford when the water is low; there appears, indeed, to be no other motive for making a road for animals to the top of the Mausoleum within the original outer wall of this tomb.

Our description begins, therefore, at the Porta del Popolo, near the Tiber on the north, and is continued to the Porta di S. Paolo, near the Tiber again on the south. There is reason to believe that the celebrated Muro Torto was part of the foundations of the palace of Sylla the dictator, which occupied all that portion of the Pincian Hill, as far as the Villa Medici, now the French Academy, and the angle of the wall beyond it. Some think this was the Villa of the Domitii. The Porta Pinciana is one of the old gateway fortresses little altered, having long been closed. The Porta Salaria has been entirely destroyed in 1871; the remains of it were, however, in a bad state, and it did not differ from the other gateways of the same period, of which several remain. These were built by Stilicho, under the Emperor Honorius, A.D. 403, and several of them were repaired and restored by King Theodoric about the year 500, as appears from his letters preserved by Cassiodorus. The most perfect of these gateway fortresses is the Porta Ostiensis, or di S. Paolo, where we have the two inner gates of the time of Claudius, the outer

* So called, because the manuscript of the ancient Itinerary, of the be- ginning of the ninth century, was found in the convent library there.

gateway with its towers, and the barbican of the time of Theodoric. The modern Porta Pia takes the place of the old Porta Nomentana, which is almost destroyed. This is near the Prætorian Camp, the northern wall of which is original, of the time of Tiberius, and very interesting. At the foot of the wall is an aqueduct, a branch of the Anio Vetus, faced with *opus reticulatum* of an early character; it was evidently made upon the old earthwork before the fine brick wall of Tiberius was built upon it. In the upper part of the same wall are remains of a *hourd*, but the marble corbels to carry this wooden balcony have been chopped off to obtain the marble, probably to burn it into lime. The east and south walls of the Prætorian Camp were rebuilt after it had been demolished by Constantine, and part of it after it had again been destroyed by the Goths. The interior of the ancient wall, with the sleeping-places for the guards in it, and other portions of this inner side, are more interesting than the outer facing.

The great corridor of Aurelian for the sentinel's path from one tower to another often remains, even where the exterior facing has been rebuilt. There are several miles of this corridor, sometimes mistaken by strangers for an aqueduct, as the conduits of the aqueducts are not unfrequently carried on arcades of similar appearance at first sight : this is especially the case between the Amphitheatrum Castrense and the Porta di S. Giovanni, where the outer wall has been destroyed, and the arcade of the corridor stands clear against the sky, so that it looks very much like an aqueduct. The finest part of the corridor is near the Porta di S. Sebastiano, the ancient Porta Appia, on both sides of which the corridor is for about half-a-mile quite perfect. On the western side of the gate, is the remarkable fresco painting of the Madonna of the sixth century, which has been preserved by the happy accident that it was over the head of the soldiers in the lofty corridor : hence it was not noticed, and has hitherto escaped observation. It may have been made by the Greek soldiers of Belisarius, or in the repairs of Theodoric.

Of the Leonine City some of the towers remain nearly perfect on the Vatican Hill above S. Peter's, now in the Pope's garden; they are very distinctly visible from the opposite hill, in ascending outside of the wall of San-Gallo, by which the Vatican fortress was connected with that on the Janiculum in the seventeenth century. The wall connecting the Vatican Palace with the castle of S. Angelo with a way on the top of it, is also perfect and extremely picturesque where it can be seen; it is, however, much concealed by modern houses and garden walls.

THE WALLS AND GATES OF ROME.

ARRANGED IN TOPOGRAPHICAL ORDER, BEGINNING AT THE NORTH END
OF ROME, THE PORTA FLAMINIA, OR DEL POPOLO.

[The numbers refer to Mr. Parker's Catalogue.]

---

*Those numbers marked with * are from drawings, valuable for historical
purposes,* but not as photographs.

1. PORTA DEL POPOLO TO PORTA
PINCIANA.

Porta del Popolo, Exterior, A.D. 1562,
(built from a design of Michael Angelo,) with the entrance to the English Chapel.　　　　1353

MURO TORTO. Part of the northern side
of the Palace of Sylla(?), B.C. 70.　1
Another view, shewing the over-
hanging wall in the lower part, and
the upper part vertical, in a series of
niches and buttresses. The construction is of rubble faced with small
diamond-shaped blocks of tufa, an
early example of Opus Reticulatum,
or net-work. The angles are formed
of oblong blocks of tufa, of nearly the
shape of modern English bricks, but
a little larger; they are often mistaken
for bricks. This wall was considered
as under the special protection of
S. Peter at the time of the siege by
the Goths, (Procopius, de Bello Gothico, ii. 29.)　　　　762

—— Palace of Sylla (?), B.C. 70. Part
of the Eastern side (now concealed
by a hideous modern wall) built to
support the earth and promenade. 2

—— Details of this, Opus Reticulatum.
On this side the wall is built in a
double series of niches, corresponding with the upper part of the northern side.　　　　1533

Towers and Wall now under the Villa
Medici : the lower part, repairs of
Belisarius, c. A.D. 520 (?), the upper
part modern.　　　　3

View from a bastion in the garden of the
French Academy, to shew an angle
of the wall and the foss-way.　1301

Palace of Sylla, B.C. 80 (?). *Plan,* with
the Muro Torto, the Porta Flaminia,
and the Piazza del Popolo.　170*

Tower of Aurelian, A.D. 275, the only
one that remains perfect.　　64

Other Towers of Aurelian (Vopiscus,
39).　　　　4

Part destroyed by the Goths, and rebuilt under Belisarius, c. A.D. 520 (?).
Under the wall is a part of the arcade
of the Aqua Virgo, the old line of
which passed along on this bank.
(Procopius, de Bello Gothico, lib. i.
c. xxiii. and lib. ii. c. ix.) This has
been *restored* in 1871.　　5

2. PORTA PINCIANA TO PORTA
SALARIA.

Porta Pinciana, Honorius, A.D. 403 (Inscription), partly rebuilt by King
Theodoric, A.D. 520 (Cassiodorus). 6.

—— Exterior, Stone Arch, A.D. 403,
Honorius (Brick Towers, Theodoric,
A.D. 520).　　　　668

—— Interior, with part of the Wall of
Aurelian, and of the Corridor for the
sentinels.　　　　1300

Two Towers near the Porta Pinciana ;
I. of Brick, of Aurelian, A.D. 275,
built on the old Mœnia ; 2. repaired
by the Popes, c. A.D. 850.　　671

Other Towers and Wall of Aurelian,
A.D. 275.　　　　670

3. PORTA SALARIA TO PORTA DI S. LORENZO,

Passing by the modern Porta Pia, the remains of the Porta Nomentana, and the Prætorian Camp.

PORTA SALARIA, Honorius, A.D. 403, see p. 198; *now destroyed.*   7

View of the Porta Pia, taken after the bombardment by the Italian troops in 1870.   1949

The breach made in the Wall near the Porta Pia by the Italian troops in 1870.   1950

Necessarium on the Wall, A.D. 850 (?), near the Porta Salaria.   669

Remains of the Porta Nomentana, Honorius, A.D. 400.   8

Postern on the outer edge of the foss of the Prætorian Camp.   9

—— Postern on the inner side of the foss.   10

PRÆTORIAN CAMP. *Plan*, according to Canina, time of Tiberius, A.D. 30 (dated by Medals).   179*

—— Northern Gate.   11

—— Details of the North Gate, with Windows of Terra Cotta.   12

—— Specus of an Aqueduct under the north Wall, with Reticulated-work of earlier character, under the brick Wall of Tiberius.   870

—— One of the Sleeping-places of the Guards in the inside of the Wall.   604

—— View of part of the Interior of the North Wall, A.D. 30, shewing the inside of a tower at the north-east angle, with part of the Corridor and sleeping-places for the Guards under the arches.   180

—— East Wall, A.D. 30, rebuilt.   13

—— Part of East Wall and Corner Tower, with corbels for a Hourd or wooden Gallery cut off, and repairs *c.* A.D. 350 (?). In the angle on the ground is shewn a wooden railing for protection against cattle in the road.   14

—— Towers at S. E. corner, shewing the construction in Opus Lateritium or brickwork of that period.   15

PRÆTORIAN CAMP (*continued*).

—— Part of the South Wall, rebuilt of the split stones of the Wall of the Kings, B.C. 550 (?), in repairs after the war with the Goths, A.D. 520. (Procopius.)   17

—— Another part of the South Wall, rebuilt of stones of the old Wall of the Kings.   16

—— Part of the South Wall, as restored after the war with the Goths, and the Gateway, called the Porta Chiusa, the outer face by Honorius, A.D. 400.   18

PORTA CHIUSA, interior, before the Excavations. Tiberius (?) altered by Honorius with older materials.   1056

—— Interior, shewing Stone Jambs of stones of the Kings, and Cornice of the Republic behind the archway of Honorius.   659

—— View of the Interior of the Porta Chiusa, *from a Drawing.*   1146*

—— Interior, as visible in 1868, shewing the early construction of the northern jamb.   1058

—— Interior, shewing the Specus of an Aqueduct (Anio Vetus?), under the southern jamb.   1057

Portion of the Wall built of Tufa blocks in the style of the Kings, rebuilt with old materials, between the Prætorian Camp and the Porta di S. Lorenzo. 965

Angle of the portion of the Stone Wall, rebuilt.   966

Interior of Wall south of the Porta Chiusa, shewing a Castellum Aquæ with the wall built across it when it was rebuilt of old materials.   1059

4. PORTA DI S. LORENZO TO THE PORTA MAGGIORE.

PORTA TIBURTINA, OR DI S. LORENZO (called Viminalis by Frontinus), Side View, exterior, the stone-work of Honorius, A.D. 403, the square brick towers rebuilt.   19

Porta Tiburtina (or di S. Lorenzo), exterior, Front View.   23

Arch of Augustus at the Porta Tiburtina, with two inscriptions of the Aqueducts, on̂e of Augustus, B.C. 3, the other of repairs ·by Caracalla, A.D. 212; the Aqueducts Marcia, Tepula, and Julia over it, (the jambs of the arch are buried by the filling up of the foss-way). 21
—— Interior, Arch of Augustus, A. U.C. 750, B.C. 3, and the inner Arch of Honorius, A.D. 403, (destroyed in 1869). 20
—— *The same, from a Drawing.* 662*
There were three arches at this gate, the original one of Augustus, to which the Emperor Honorius added a *barbican* or gateway fortress, with an inner and outer gate ; the inner gate of these three has now been destroyed.
—— *Plan* of the Gate with the Aqueducts and the Castellum Aquæ Tepulæ. 1238*
—— *Plan* of the Wall and Aqueducts and fortress of Honorius. 23*
—— *Plan* of the Gate with the neighbourhood, shewing the line of the Aqueducts and remains of the Reservoirs of the Tepula and Julia in the Wall of Rome. 1111*
—— Section, shewing the different levels of the roads, and of the Aqueducts. 1291*
—— Transverse section. 1296*
Towers near the Porta Tiburtina, rebuilt A.D. 1450. 24
Castellum Aquæ Tepulæ, rebuilt by Trajan, built on the old Agger, and incorporated in the Wall, with corbels for a Hourd, or wooden Gallery. 25
Ancient Postern between the Porta S. Lorenzo and the Porta Maggiore, supposed by some to be the Porta Collatina. 27

5. PORTA MAGGIORE TO PORTA ASINARIA.
Porta Prænestina and Labicana, or Maggiore (called by Frontinus, Esquilina), Exterior, A.D. 80, and the Baker's Tomb. 30

Porta Prænestina, from the north, shewing the Conduits of the Aqueducts. 31
—— The same, from the north-east, with the Aqueducts over it. 32
—— Transverse section, shewing the Aqueducts, &c. 1463*
The SESSORIUM, now S. Croce in Gerusalemme. *The Plan,* with the eastern angle of the Wall, the Aqueduct of Claudius and Nero, the Porta Maggiore, the Amphitheatrum Castrense, Porta Asinaria, &c. 33*
—— Part of the Wall outside of the Sessorium, with the lower part of a Tower rebuilt of Tufa. 413
Amphitheatrum Castrense, c. A.D. 100. 34
South Wall near the Sessorium. Aurelian, A.D. 275, exterior, on an older *agger,* with repairs. 35
—— Interior of the same, shewing the Corridor for the sentinels and the inner side of one of the towers. 36
Interior of the Corridor, now in the garden of S. Croce in Gerusalemme. 414
Exterior of Wall and Towers, c. A.D. 275, built upon the old Mœnia near the Sessorium. 415
—— Another portion, built upon earlier work of stone. 416
—— Another portion of the Wall, near the Porta Asinaria. 573

6. PORTA ASINARIA TO PORTA DI S. SEBASTIANO,
Passing by the Lateran Palace and Gate, the Porta Metronia and P. Latina.

Porta S. Giovanni, A.D. 1574, (with the embrasure for cannon in the year 1868.) 1319
PORTA ASINARIA, exterior, Aurelian, A.D. 275. 37
Interior, A.D. 275, and repairs, A.D. 403. 417
Porta Asinaria and Porta S. Giovanni, from the mill on the Marrana, on the southern side of Rome. 1318
—— Curious Medieval Sculpture in bas-relief of the Porta Asinaria and the ancient Lateran, now in the sacristy of that church. 1726

Wall across the Foss of the Lateran Palace, on the northern side, built by Belisarius (?)   39

View of a portion of the Lateran Palace, A.D. 50, included in the Wall of Aurelian.   173

LATERAN PALACE. Eastern angle, much mutilated.   41

—— Remains of another part of the House of Plautius Lateranus, incorporated in the City Wall.   571

—— Lateran Palace, Plan, with part of the Wall of Aurelian.   38*

PORTA LATÉRANENSIS, Arch of the Gate now closed.   40

—— Arch, as excavated in 1868.   1096

—— Wall or Jamb of the Gate (?) or Postern (?), and portion of an earlier Tomb.   1097

—— *The same, from a Drawing.*   1149*

—— The Lateran from the Marrana, shewing the position of the Porta Lateranensis in the angle.   1309

Tower of Aurelian near the Lateran, A.D. 275, with stones of the Wall of the Kings built up against the foot of it by Belisarius (removed A.D. 1869). "Having only a short time to repair the walls, he collected the stones which were lying near, and used them in a tumultuous manner." (Procopius, de Bello Gothico, lib. iii. c. 24.)   42

Two Towers near the Lateran, one of brick of Aurelian, A.D. 275, the other built of stones of the Wall of the Kings, B.C. 650.   43

PORTA METRONIA, interior, A.D. 275, with repairs, A.D. 1157, shewing also part of the Corridor of Aurelian, A.D. 275.   44

—— Interior, with Inscription, recording repairs by the Senate, A.D. 1157.   45

—— Within the Walls, View on the south side.   1217

Towers between the Porta Metronia and Porta Latina, with substructions.   875

Corridor for the Sentinels within the Wall.   1216

PORTA LATINA, exterior, Honorius, A.D. 403, and Belisarius, A.D. 535 (?), or Theodoric, A.D. 500.   46

Interior, Honorius, A.D. 403, with the Chapel of S. John in Olio, A.D. 1520.   47

—— Another View.   567

—— Interior of side Tower.   1361

7. PORTA APPIA, OR DI S. SEBASTIANO, TO THE PORTA OSTIENSIS, OR DI S. PAOLO.

General View of the exterior of the Wall, near the Porta di S. Sebastiano.   48

PORTA APPIA, now di S. Sebastiano, Honorius, A.D. 403, partly rebuilt, and brick towers added by King Theodoric, c. A.D. 520.   49

—— Interior, with Arch of Drusus in the foss-way, A.D. 30.   50

—— View of the West Side within the Walls, shewing the difference of level when compared with the view outside the Walls.   1204

—— Interior of part of the western Tower, the lower part stonework of Honorius, A.D. 403, the upper part brickwork of Theodoric, A.D. 520.   1205

Interior of the Wall of Aurelian, between the Porta Ardeatina and the Porta Appia, shewing the Corridor for the sentinels and the inside of the Towers.   1206

Corridor for the Sentinels, with the Porta Appia in the distance.   1215

Marble Steps in the Corridor, probably repairs of the time of Theodoric.   1207

Corridor for the Sentinels, with Fresco-painting of the Madonna, c. A.D. 520.   1208

PORTA ARDEATINA, c. A.D. 60. Exterior.   565

—— Interior.   566

—— Specus of an Aqueduct in the interior of the Wall at the Porta Ardeatina, north-east side.   986

Bastion of Sangallo, A. D. 1540, parts of the Casemate in the interior.

1210, 1211, 1212
—— Junction of the Bastion of Sangallo, with the Wall of Aurelian near the Aventine, from above.   1218
—— *Plan and Sections* of parts near the Bastion of Sangallo, shewing the difference of the levels within and without.   1292*

Interior of a Tower on the Aventine, between the Bastion of Sangallo and the Porta S. Paolo, rebuilt in the fourth century, and again in the Middle Ages, as shewn by the construction.   1213

Tower near the Aventine and S. Sabba, interior, rebuilt in the Middle Ages.   1214

Initials and Arms of Nicholas V., in brick, A. D. 1450.   973

Interior on the Pseudo-Aventine, shewing part of the Brick Wall and one of the Towers of Aurelian, A. D. 275, built against the cliff of the hill.   223

Interior of part of the Corridor and Tower, built upon older work.   363

Interior of a Tower and part of the Corridor.   267

Perspective View from the Pseudo-Aventine to the Tiber, with the Porta Ostiensis or S. Paolo and the pyramid of Caius Cestius. This part of the wall is built in the bottom of the great foss.   140

8. PORTA OSTIENSIS TO THE TIBER.

PORTA OSTIENSIS, now di S. Paolo, Honorius, exterior, A. D. 403, partly rebuilt by King Theodoric, *c.* A. D. 520.   51
—— Interior, Theodoric, A. D. 520, the two arches earlier.   52
—— Details of the Fortifications, Theodoric, A. D. 520.   53
—— Interior of Battlements, Theodoric, A. D. 520.   54
—— Corridor, with Parapet and Battlements, Theodoric, A. D. 520.   55

PORTA OSTIENSIS (*continued*).
—— *Plans* of the two Stories.   350*
—— *Plan* of the Gateway and the neighbourhood.   1294*
—— Section of the Gateway and Towers, with the Pyramid of Caius Cestius and Pavement of the Via Ostiensis. 1293*

Ruined Towers between the Porta Ostiensis, now di S. Paolo, and the Tiber, A. D. 850 and 1450.   56
—— Ruined Tower at the Angle next the Tiber, A. D. 850.   57

9. THE TRASTEVERE.

PORTA PORTESE OR PORTUENSIS. 1305
Ruins of part of the Wall of Aurelian on the south side of the Janiculum, Exterior.   955
—— Interior.   954
—— Interior of a Tower of Aurelian, between the Janiculum and the Tiber.   952

Foss of the Janiculum, from near S. Pietro in Montorio, looking down.   957

Inner Foss of the Janiculum, south side, looking upwards.   953

Foss of the Janiculum, south side, from below, taken in 1867, before the erection of the new battery.   956

Tower in the Garden of the Villa Corsini in Trastevere, between the Janiculum and the Porta Settimiana, with medieval repairs.   949

Wall between the Porta Settimiana and the Janiculum, Interior.   951

PORTA SETTIMIANA in Trastevere as rebuilt, *c.* A. D. 1450.   1306, 1075

Tower of Aurelian in the Trastevere, between the Porta Settimiana and the Tiber, A. D. 275.   945

Second Tower of Aurelian, between the Porta Settimiana and the Tiber. 948

Tower of Aurelian in the Trastevere, near the Tiber, A. D. 275.   946

Construction of a Tower of Aurelian, A. D. 275, near the Porta Settimiana.   947

North End of the Wall of Aurelian in the Tiber, near Ponte Sisto, on the Trastevere side.   1036

Towers in the Tiber, near S. Giovanni
de' Fiorentini.   919
Vatican Fortress, Scarped Cliff of the
time of the Kings, on the south side,
near Porta S. Spirito.   958
Scarped Cliff of the Vatican, and Wall
of Sangallo built upon it, near the
Porta S. Spirito.   959
Wall of the Leonine City, exterior,
A. D. 850.   1312
—— Loop-hole, A. D. 850.   962

The Tower of the Winds enclosed in
the Walls of Urban VIII.   225
PORTA S. SPIRITO, by Sangallo, in the
Borgo, or Leonine City.   1455
PORTA CAVALLEGGIERI in the Leonine
City.   1313
PORTA ANGELICA in the Borgo, or
Leonine City, A.D. 1540, with the
Vatican Palace in the background,
(and an embrasure for cannon,) in
1868.   1354

The Porta Salaria was destroyed in 1871 by the municipal architect, in the course of what he calls the *restoration* of the Wall. Some
interesting tombs of the first century were found buried in the round
towers of Honorius, in the same manner as the Baker's tomb had
been found at the Porta Maggiore in 1833.

Tomb of Sulpicius Maximus.   2070
Tomb resembling that of Bibulus.   2069
Circular Tomb faced with Opus Reticulatum.   2071

CONSTRUCTION OF WALLS.

PREFACE.

THE manner of constructing walls at different periods is of the greatest importance for the elucidation of the history of architecture, more especially in Rome, where the difference of construction of each period is so very marked. Even in England and France it is usual for experienced eyes to read off the date of a building at sight, within twenty years. In Rome, the distinctions are so much more broad and marked, that it is far more easy. The great oblong blocks of tufa mark the time of the Kings, the massive walls of concrete or rubble mark that of the Republic, and the concrete with the surface faced with brick, or reticulated work, or marble, that of the early Empire, each as a rough general rule. In England, the mouldings are considered as the only safe guide to the date of a building, but the construction should be considered also, no one feature can be depended on by itself. The same mouldings are often used again, when the church has had a vault with a clerestory added, as was frequently the case in the latter part of the twelfth century and the beginning of the thirteenth. In Rome, we have to do with buildings perhaps fifteen hundred years older than any we have in England, and although the same habit of careful observation applies everywhere, in the earlier period we have no mouldings at all, unless a flat projecting cornice or string-course can be so called. We must therefore rely on the construction only, and then we must always bear in mind the quarries from which the stone was taken ; but as in Rome we know that the early Romans had not access to any quarries but those in Rome itself, or the immediate neighbourhood, for the first hundred years, we may expect that where we find *tufa* alone used, and a rude mode of construction without mortar (for lime-stone also was very scarce in that district), we have to do with buildings of the first century of Rome. After the conquest of Alba Longa, at about the end of that century, *peperino* was added from the quarries in the Alban hills. After the lapse of another century, the *sperone* came in from the quarries at Gabii, in the time of the Tarquins, and the early part of the Republic. The excellent lime-stone called *travertine*, from the quarries at Tivoli, did not come into general use in Rome until four centuries later, and was soon followed by marble from more distant countries. Independently of these building materials, which it is not always easy to distinguish at first sight, the construction itself is a sufficient guide, and we can see the difference when it has been once pointed out, between the wide vertical joints of the early period, into which a cane can be thrust, and the closely-fitted joints and well-cut stone of the second period, and the iron clamps, or the holes from which they have fallen, in the third period.

The distinction between the large blocks of the time of the Kings, and the rough walls of the Republic, and the brick, and marble, and reticulated work of the Empire, is obvious to a mere child, when he has once been shewn that each is the mark of a particular period of history. When we come to the Empire, the different thickness of the bricks is also very obvious when once pointed out : we have good historical types of each century as a guide. We know that the reticulated-work is not found after the time of Hadrian, and that the very fine brick-work also ceases at that time. There is no place like Rome for the number of historical and dated examples of each change in the fashion of construction to serve as types, and this has been well said to be the basis of all archæology, the foundation upon which it was all built. The remarkable thing is, that so little attention has hitherto been paid to that point. The present work is believed to be the first in which any attention has been given to it.

During the Medieval period, Rome was very much behind the west of Europe in construction, and it is therefore of secondary importance; at best it was only a good imitation of that of the early Empire, and most of the buildings were constructed only of old materials worked up again. The struggles and difficulties from which the medieval style originated were unknown in Rome, where old materials were always over abundant. The miserable result, in an architectural point of view, is well known,—the medieval buildings of Rome are contemptible in construction.

HISTORICAL PHOTOGRAPHS
ILLUSTRATIVE OF THE CONSTRUCTION OF WALLS.

[The numbers refer to Mr. Parker's Catalogue.]

TYPICAL EXAMPLES.

*Those marked with * are from drawings, valuable for historical purposes,*
but not as photographs.

TIME OF THE KINGS.
OPUS QUADRATUM.

Wall of Romulus on the Palatine, B.C. 750? (Livii Hist., lib. i. c. 11.) 779
"Quadrata saxa . . . sunt enim circa Urbem." (Vitruv., de Archit., lib. ii. c. 7.)

Tabularium on the Capitol, the ancient part, B.C. 730. 2646
"Ejus vestigia nunc manent tria . . . quod post Ædem Saturni in ædificiorum legibus," &c. (T. Varro, de Ling. Lat., lib. v. c. 7.)

Wall of the Kings (A.U.C. 189, B.C. 564; Livii Hist., i. 36) in the Forum of Augustus, and Wall of Travertine between that Forum and the Forum Transitorium of Nerva, A.D. 96, inserted in the old wall of tufa. 844
"Numa built one temple common, to them all, between the Capitoline and Palatine hills. Both these hills had already been encompassed *with one wall.*" (Dionys., Hist., lib. i. c. 66.)

Interior of a Tower by the side of the Circus Maximus, at the foot of the Palatine, probably part of the wall that enclosed the Palatine and the hill of Saturn as one city, afterwards used for the Pulvinarium of the Circus Maximus. 748
"Loca divisa patribus equitibusque." (Livii Hist., lib. i. c. 35.)

Wall of the Kings on the Aventine, near S. Prisca, probably built by the Latins when settled there. (Livii Hist., lib. i. c. 33, and iii. 50.) 829

MAMERTINE PRISON—Lower Wall of Tufa, time of Ancus Martius. 848
"Ancus . . . Carcer . . . in media urbe imminens foro ædificavit." (Livii Hist., lib. i. c. 33.)
"Ut frangendi carceris . . . delegatum in Tullianum." (Ibid., lib. xxix. c. 22.)
"Lautumiæ . . . carceris Lautumiarum." (Ibid., lib. xxxii. c. 26.)
"In inferiorem carcerem." (Ibid., lib. xxxiv. c. 44.)

Wall of Servius Tullius. (Livii Hist., lib. i. c. 36; Plinii Nat. Hist., xxxvi. 24. 3.) * 793

TIME OF THE REPUBLIC.
CONCRETE. FARTURA.

Concrete (*fartura, opera a sacco*) in layers, in a Fort under S. Saba, B.C. 300 (?). 993
This wall is faced with blocks of tufa in the style of the Kings in the lower part, now underground, as was shewn in some excavations in 1870.

Early Concrete Wall on the Palatine, B.C. 300 (?). 991
"Intrinsecus quæ medio calcato farturis." (Vitruvius, lib. ii. c. viii.)

OPUS INCERTUM.

Arch in the Emporium, B.C. 175. (Livii Hist., lib. xli. c. 32.) 990

Wall of a House of the time of the Republic, B.C. 100 (?), on the Viminal. 2082
"Antiquum quod incertum dicitur." (Vitruvius, lib. ii. c. 8.)

TIME OF THE EMPIRE.

OPUS RETICULATUM—NET-WORK.

Muro Torto, B.C. 100(?). 781
House of Nero, A.D. 60. (Plinii Nat.
  Hist., lib. xxxvii. c. 24. 5. 7.) 1285
Villa of Hadrian, at Tivoli, A.D. 120.
  899
  "Reticulatum quod nunc omnes
utuntur." (Vitruvius, lib. ii. c. 8.)

OPUS LATERITIUM—BRICKWORK.

Cornice and Window in the Pantheum
  of Agrippa, B.C. 26. (Dion Cassius,
  lib. liii. c. 27.) 1237
House of Nero, with flat brick Arches.
  326
Capital and Cornice, Amphitheatrum
  Castrense, A.D. 135. 994
Thermæ of Antoninus Caracalla, A.D.
  212. (Spartianus, c. 9.) . 978

TRAVERTINE, OR MARBLE.

Facing to the Tomb of Cæcilia Metella,
  B.C. 103. (Inscription.) 979
Temple of Fortuna Virilis, A.D. 10.
  (Taciti Annales, lib. ii. c. 44.) 976
Arcade of the Mamertine Prison, in the
  Forum of Julius Cæsar, A.D. 22.
  (Inscription.) 778

Temple of Antoninus and Faustina
  A.D. 161. (Medal and Inscription.)
  975

FOURTH CENTURY. DECADENCE.

Villa Quintilii, on the Via Appia. 1134
Circus of Maxentius, A.D. 310. 977

MEDIEVAL BRICK-WORK.

Arcade, S. Stefano Rotondo, with a
  Byzantine Capital, A.D. 461. 995
House of S. Gregory on the Cœlian,
  A.D. 590. 996
Church of S. Hadrian in the Forum
  Romanum, A.D. 626. (Anastasius,
  Honorius, 120.) 998
Apse of the Church of S. John, at the
  Porta Latina, A.D. 1120, and Wall
  of Church, A.D. 772. 999

OPERA SARACENESCA.

Campanile of the Church of S. Rocco,
  at Frascati, A.D. 1305. 709
Monastery of S. Sisto Vecchio, Rome.
  974

ADDITIONAL EXAMPLES[*].

OPUS QUADRATUM.

Wall at Lanuvium, B.C. 800 (Livii Hist., lib. i. c. I, et lib. iii. c. 29), now Civita Lavinia. 2386

Tusculum—Construction of Opus Quadratum, west side, *c.* B.C. 800 (Livii Hist., lib. i. c. I). 1900

Fiesole—Etruscan Wall built of split tufa, corresponding with the Wall of Romulus in Rome. 517

Vico-Varo — Wall of large stones of early character,—called Cyclopean. 1569

Wall of the time of the Kings, on the Aventine (of the Latins?), A.U.C. 114, B.C. 639 (Livii Hist., lib. i. c. 33, et lib. iii. c. 58). 749

THE SECOND PERIOD.

Wall of the Circus Maximus, A.U.C. 30, B.C. 109 (?). 780

Wall of the Kings, A.U.C. 30—60 (?), B.C. 723—693 (?), in the Forum of Augustus, of the enclosure of the Palatine and Hill of Saturn in one City. 881

Tabularium, east end, with Doorway bearing Inscription, B.C. 35. 577, 578

Wall of Servius Tullius, B.C. 564, near the Railway Station (destroyed in 1870). 792

Mamertine Prison—Walls of Tufa, time of Ancus Martius, A.U.C. 121, B.C. 631. 849

THIRD PERIOD, A.U.C. 100, B.C. 200 (?).

Temple of Spes in the Forum Olitorium, B.C. 524 (?), or B.C. 261 (?). 1231

Temple of Juno Sospita in the Forum Olitorium, B.C. 194. 1230
(Livii Hist., lib. xxxiv. c. 53, in the Church of S. Nicolas in Carcere.)

Temple of Pietas, B.C. 180. 1229
(Livii Hist., lib. i. c. 84), in the Forum Olitorium.

FARTURA OR CONCRETE.

Muro Torto, B.C. 80 (?). 992

Villa of Hadrian, at Tivoli, A.D. 120. 900

OPUS RETICULATUM.

Mausoleum of Augustus, B.C. 28. 987

Tomb on the Via Ardeatina, time of Sylla, *c.* B.C. 80. 1182

Part of a Tomb, *c.* A.D. 100. 1942

From an Aqueduct (the Anio Vetus, as rebuilt by Trajan, near Tivoli). 950

—— Reservoir of the first century, in the Thermæ of the Gordiani. 927

Tusculum—House of Cicero, B.C. 20. 1894 & 1895

Domus Hortorum Domitii. 2107

TRAVERTINE.

On the Esquiline, near S. Pietro in Vincoli. 800

Mamertine Prison, the part rebuilt, A.D. 22, with Inscription. 580

SPERONE. LAPIS GABINUS.

Arco di Pantano, in the Forum of Augustus. 1465

OPUS LATERITIUM.

FIRST CENTURY.

Doorway and Window of a shop of the first century, in the Infima nova Via (T. Varro), called the street of Julius Cæsar, at the foot of the Palatine on the side of the Circus Maximus. (Plinii Nat. Hist., lib. xxxvi. c. 24.) 746

Lateritium and Reticulatum—House of Nero. 1252

Arches of Nero on the Cœlian. 78

House of Pudens, *c.* A.D. 60. 178

Hall of Lateran Palace, with Arches of a peculiar kind. 174

Tomb on the Via Appia Nova. 1037

[*] Examples of the Construction of Walls are endless, those selected are characteristic of their respective periods.

Tomb over the Catacomb of the Jews, in the Via Appia. 1755
Palace of Domitian on the Palatine, A.D. 85. 1756
Tombs on the Via Latina. 1430 & 1431
Nero, A.D. 57, and Trajan, A.D. 100, in the house of Nero. 1400
Arches of the first century (?) on the Palatine. 1127

SECOND CENTURY.

Doorway of the Thermæ of Trajan, A.D. 110, now in the Church of SS. Martino e Silvestro in Monti. 1341
Arches of Vaults and Doorways in the House of Pudens, as altered in the second century.
2074, 2075, 2076, 2077
Angle of Wall of the Prætorium, c. A.D. 160, now in the Church of S. Croce in Gerusalemme. 405

THIRD CENTURY.

Pediment, called of the Colossus of Nero, but really of the time of Septimius Severus, A.D. 220. 786
Meta Sudans, originally built A.D. 80 (?), rebuilt A.D. 220. 1744
Arch of the Circus Alexandrinus, A.D. 230, now in the Piazza Navona. 1162

FIFTH CENTURY.

Clerestory of the Church of SS. John and Paul, A.D. 417. 397

NINTH CENTURY.

Wall of Monastery of SS. Martin and Silvester, A.D. 860. 1325

TWELFTH CENTURY.

Monastery of S. Clement—Wall, with small round Windows. 938

IT is impossible to understand the archæology of Rome without studying the Aqueducts. In every part of the City, and of the country round it, there are remains of them; they are frequently mistaken for something else, and called by other names, misleading those who have not given attention to the subject. They are necessarily mixed up with the *Thermæ*, for most of the aqueducts were made to bring water to those great establishments. There was also a reservoir of water supplied by the aqueducts under each of the palaces, larger houses and villas, as may be seen in many parts of the Palatine, under the palaces of the Cæsars. In their original state the Aqueducts must have been among the grandest objects in Rome, and the most conspicuous in all directions. The principal approach from the east passed between two fine arcades of the aqueducts, one carrying three of them, the other two. These two fine arcades were not more than a hundred yards apart; all the great roads from the eastern side were brought into this space, and certainly, for the last mile into Rome, must have had one of these arcades on either hand: to the left, or south, the Claudian arcade, fifty feet high; to the right, the Marcian, thirty feet high.

For the last half-mile, the Claudian arcade was also the boundary of the palace gardens of the Sessorium, the residence first of the Kings and afterwards of one branch of the imperial family (that of Verus or Varius), who resided there for more than a century. That portion of the arcade still exists for a considerable extent, forming the northern wall of that garden, and at the same time part of the wall of the city, Aurelian having adopted it, and incorporated it with his great wall. This portion is thoroughly shewn in my Photographs, as it is a very important part of the antiquities of Rome, and illustrates many points. It was the place where the principal aqueducts entered Rome, and the whole ground is full of remains of them with their reservoirs and filtering-places. The inner side of the wall is the part necessarily shewn, because the outer side is concealed by the arcade of the Aqua Felice, excepting in places where the *specus* of the Claudia and the Anio Novus appear above it. Just outside of this garden, at the west end of it, is the great foss which

separated the Sessorium, or fortified palace, from the other fortifications of the City, and in it are remains of the two great
reservoirs that were probably the Gemelli or Twins of Frontinus,
made originally for the Appia and the Anio Vetus side by side,
and used afterwards to receive the surplus water of the later
aqueducts on a higher level. We then have a considerable number
of the Arches of Nero, following a straight line for another mile
to the west end of the Cœlian Hill; where remains of the great
reservoir are on a level with the *specus* carried on the top of this
arcade, fifty feet above the ground in that high situation, from which
the water was distributed in all directions, first on other arcades,
three of which branched off from this point, and afterwards in .metal
pipes when it was sub-divided; but for the main supply no metal
pipes then to be had were large and strong enough to bear the
pressure of a stream of water four feet deep and two feet wide,
running at the rate of five or six miles an hour, if not more. The
direct line went on over the Palatine to the Capitol, passing over
the Forum Romanum on the bridge of Caligula, of which, also,
some remains are shewn in my Photographs; the other two branches
from the great reservoir over the Arch of Dolabella, went one to
the right to the Colosseum (to supply the Stagna there), the other
to the left to the Aventine, to supply the private house of Trajan
and the Thermæ of Sura.

The Porta Maggiore stood at the end of the long vista between
the two great aqueducts, and was itself made out of two of the arches
of the Claudian arcade, in the last of the angles that occurred at
every half-mile. The penultimate one was at the eastern end of
the Sessorium palace gardens, where this water entered Rome,
and then, after passing the angle to the north, with the usual
piscina and *castellum aquæ*, or reservoir and filtering-place, turned
again to the west, as far as that gate where the Claudian arcade
terminated. From this point the Marcian turned to the north
upon the great bank of earth which formed the outer defence of
Rome in that part, and continued along it for another half-mile,
as far as the Porta di S. Lorenzo, and beyond it to the Prætorian
Camp; then turning again to the west, it went across the great inner
foss between the outer bank, the great *agger* of Servius Tullius, which
formed the inner line, where remains of it were found near the railway station in 1871, with inscriptions on two of the *cippi*, stating that
the three aqueducts passed there. It is not quite correct to say
that the *arcades* were carried there, because where the ground is
high the *specus* are carried underground. This is the case between

the Porta Maggiore (the Porta Esquilina of Frontinus) and the Porta di S. Lorenzo (the Porta Viminalis of the same). The *specus* is seen on arches close to each of the gates; but, between the two, it passed underground through a sort of hillock, about midway between the two gates, as is mentioned by Frontinus. The ground is high again near the Porta Chiusa at the Prætorian Camp, and in the great bank or *agger* of Servius Tullius.

These two great arcades are those chiefly known to visitors to Rome as THE AQUEDUCTS; but the underground aqueducts are at least equally interesting when understood. The Anio Vetus being near the surface can be traced all over Rome; the Appia being very deep, is not so easily traced, and can only be seen with certainty near its source and its mouth. There are other arcades nearly as fine as these; but, as they do not come so near Rome, they are less known; in the parts nearest to the City they are either underground or destroyed. One of them is that called Alexandrina by Fabretti; but the original parts of it are of the time of Hadrian and Trajan. This runs from the source near Gabii and Labicum, now la Colonna, to the place called *Cento-Celle.* Possibly some of the hundred cells or vaults found there and supposed to have been all tombs, were really reservoirs of water. At every great villa there are always remains of these great cisterns for the supply of water, and this is about three miles from Rome, where a great villa of Hadrian was situated. This arcade extends for miles across the country between the two great roads, one from Gabii, the other from Preneste (now Palestrina). Another fine arcade is seen on the road to Albano, at the Tor di Mezza Via (or half-way house). This has been ascertained to be the Aqua Aurelia, which goes to the villa of the Quintilii on the Via Appia, and from thence into Rome to supply the Thermæ of Commodus and Severus, of which also remains have been found; the latter part of its course is chiefly underground.

It was very difficult at first to ascertain to which of the aqueducts each of the remains belonged that were seen on all sides; and I found it necessary to follow each aqueduct up to its source, and then down to its mouth, in order to ascertain this. This work has taken me some years, in connection with the other branches of the general subject of the Archæology of Rome. It has now been done, with one exception,—the aqueduct made to bring water to the Thermæ of Diocletian on the Viminal,—which has not been traced; but there is great probability that it was a branch from one of the older aqueducts, probably brought across from the great reservoir where the

Nymphæum of Alexander Severus was situated, on which the Trophies of Marius were hung. This is on high ground, and at a short distance only, so that it would be very convenient for the purpose. We see that there are several branches from that point, and one of them probably supplied these great Thermæ, for which purpose more than one aqueduct would be tapped. It may be that the curious sort of tower reservoir—long supposed to have been a tomb, a short distance to the south of the Trophies of Marius— was the one for these Thermæ; in either case, these reservoirs were supplied from the great old aqueducts.

I may almost say that wherever the aqueducts are visible, they can now be seen in my Photographs, and in some places the remains have been destroyed since these were taken, during what is called the *Restoration* of the City Walls. Perhaps the finest and most interesting part of the Aqueducts are the great cascades at the source of the Anio Novus above Subiaco, in the bed of that river, situated in some of the finest scenery in the world. Among later works the ingenious manner in which the bed of the small river Almo is made use of to carry the water of two other mountain streams, the Aqua Crabra and the Marrana, the water of which never fails ; and the manner in which the tunnel of the Aqua Julia has been used again in the twelfth century, are the most curious and interesting. This had hitherto escaped observation, and was not easily traced. The Aqua Felice was unfortunately carried out in a very rude manner ; the plan of the Pope was a good one, but was spoiled by the ignorance of the engineer.

The new aqueduct, the Aqua Marcia-Pia, restoring the celebrated Aqua Marcia to use in Rome, is a work deserving of high commendation. It is much to be regretted that my lamented friend the late Mr. Shepherd, to whose energy and perseverance we are chiefly indebted for this, did not live to see the completion of his work. Much credit is also due to Signor Moraldi, the originator of the scheme, to whom the Company still pay a premium, which he well deserves. His map[*] of the Aqua Marcia, of which he kindly gave

---

[*] During the first season that I was resident in Rome, it was my habit to go with my friend Mr. William Long, of Balliol College, Oxford, then resident in Rome, into the Catacombs every Monday morning, and along the line of the Aqueducts also once or twice a-week, when the weather permitted. We procured all the best maps of the Campagna that were to be had, but could find none that would enable us to trace the course of the Aqueducts. Moltke's map is the best as far as it goes ; but, being intended as a military map only, he paid no attention to the antiquities. The one known in England by the name of Gell, and in Rome by the name of Nibby, is made especially for the Antiquities ; but it is on a small scale, and we found it impossible to trace the Aqueducts upon it. Eventually I have had one made on a large scale,

me a photograph, was of great service to me, as far as it went; but I saw it was necessary to go further, and include all the Aqueducts on the eastern side of Rome. I was fortunate in meeting with Dr. Fabio Gori, who is a native of Subiaco, and has been interested in the Aqueducts from his boyhood. He shewed me that Signor Moraldi had not gone quite far enough, and that the real spring of the Marcia is about a mile further from Rome than the one he supposed to be so, which was a subsidiary spring, though of equally good water. At the original source the stone *specus* was found, having been long concealed by being a foot or two under water. I saw it, and stood upon it, and had a photograph made, so that there could be no mistake, and the engineer of the company also saw it, and carried his aqueduct to that point; so that the real ancient Aqua Marcia now comes into Rome again, and is getting rapidly into general use, being much the best drinking water. The water supply of ancient Rome has long been a subject of interest, and can now be more perfectly understood than it ever could before. The series of Photographs of them are a thorough illustration of their history, such as could not have been made before that art was invented.

to make it clear, have added the other Antiquities, and then had it reduced by photography to two smaller sizes: one very small, to give the general lines only; the other on a size convenient for the pocket; and, by using the portion near Rome separately, it makes a good and convenient map for the purpose.

HISTORICAL PHOTOGRAPHS OF THE AQUEDUCTS.

[*The numbers refer to Mr. Parker's Catalogue.*]

---

*Those marked with * are from drawings, valuable for historical purposes,*
but not as photographs.

In his admirable treatise on the Aqueducts, Frontinus mentions in his first book, as an introduction, that before they were made, the Roman people, for the space of 441 years after the foundation of the City, were content with the water from the Tiber and from certain natural springs which from their salubrity were supposed to be sanctified.

One of the springs, called Aqua Argentina, deserves special attention ; it comes out of the rock in a considerable body, and with much force, under the north-west corner of the Palatine Hill, at a great depth, in the cave called the Lupercal, which from its situation may very well have been a wolf's cave at the time of the foundation of Rome. (702* is the plan and section of this). It falls into the larger stream that comes from the Quirinal and Capitoline Hills, and now runs in the Cloaca Maxima (690*). The point of junction of these two streams can be seen in an opening where the vault has been destroyed (158), near the arch of Janus and the church of S. Georgio in Velabro, which was the silversmiths' quarter in Rome, as is shewn by the arch they erected in honour of Septimius Severus near this spot, the inscription on which remains.

The stream that comes from the foot of the Quirinal, and now runs through the Cloaca Maxima, emerges in a cellar under a house at the back of the church of S. Hadrian, and

a great body of water rises with considerable force. Such a spring is no doubt in its original place. Another spring that runs into this stream is the one that rises in the crypt under the church of the Crucifixion, at the foot of the Capitoline Hill, called the Prison of S. Peter, which is another natural source.

Of the wells or reservoirs of rainwater, we have one remarkable example still preserved ; it is on the Palatine Hill, at the north-west corner, just behind the most perfect part of the Wall of Romulus, and at one corner of his *arx* or citadel, called Roma Quadrata, and there are certain peculiarities about it. It has *specus*, or subterranean conduits, to carry water to it from different parts of the hill. The cistern itself is seven feet high, of about the same width, and of considerable length. Into this reservoir descend certain wells of a peculiar and unusual form, like a hollow cone with the wide mouth downwards. This form of well is said to be common in the east ; but the only examples known in this part of Italy are this one on the Palatine under the *arx* of Romulus, and one at Alba Longa, under the corner of the *arx* or citadel of that ancient city, from which the Romans are said to have been originally a colony. This is certainly a remarkable coincidence, if it is nothing more. One of these wells is shewn in 764 and 765 from nature, and in 366*,

384*, from a drawing. 1630 is a view of the reservoir at Alba Longa (miscalled the Prison). 1940* is from a drawing of the two compared.

The remains of the aqueduct and reservoir at Tusculum (shewn in 1903) are of *opus quadratum*, of very early character, and seem to shew that the inhabitants there had aqueducts before the Romans. Frontinus, indeed, makes no claim to invention, nor were the Romans generally inventors, they rather turned to useful account the inventions of other people whom they had conquered.

I. THE APPIA—was made by the Censor, Appius Claudius Crassus (Cæcus[a]), in the year of Rome 441, B.C. 312, and has its origin in and near to the Latomiæ or Stone Quarries of the time of the Kings of Rome, on the bank of the river Anio, in which one of the sources of this aqueduct is found.   865, 866, 867

The Caves of Cervaro are a continuation of these Quarries, shewn in 1557.

1155* and 1968* are plans of the sources of the Aqua Appia and Aqua Virgo, in the Meadows of Lucullus, near Collatia.

These meadows are now known by the medieval towers called La Rustica, Sapienza (1551), and Cervaro (1552), and the lines of the aqueduct, crossing them from different springs and meeting in a central reservoir, can be traced by the clumps of shrubs over each well. The aqueduct itself being at a great depth, but still having water in it for the greater part of the year, and moisture always, the line of these wells is thus distinguished. From the central reservoir, in which the water was collected, the *Specus* or Conduit was carried into Rome, always at a great depth.

The spring of the Augustan branch (added A.D. 10) is found under a cottage (1550), near the town or castle of Cervelletta.

The *Specus*, or Conduit of each of the aqueducts, is distinguished by a slight change of form, and often of size also. Sections of fifteen of these are given in the map, and shewn in the photographs of it, 1982*. That of the Appia being the lowest, and always at a great depth, has been the most difficult to distinguish; but within the walls of Rome it passed along the Cœlian Hill[b] (691*, 890*), and then across the short space between the Cœlian and the Aventine, upon the bank or Agger of Servius Tullius (1100, 1136, 1164, 1165, 1289, 1288, 1166), and very near to (*proxima*) the Porta Capena (1138*). After passing the Piscina Publica, and serving as a drain for the surplus water, it is continued at the foot of the cliff of the Pseudo-Aventine, under S. Balbina and S. Sabba, to the mouth of it (84*) on the bank of the Tiber, under the Priorato near the Marmorata and the Porta Trigemina. The *specus* is here distinctly visible, filled up with the clay deposit to one-third of its height (1116); the view in the stone quarry and a section of one of the wells is shewn in 889*. A Plan of the stone quarry under S. Sabba shews several aqueducts meeting in it, and throwing their surplus water into the

---

[a] See Frontinus de Aqueductibus, c. 5.

[b] There is a large and deep reservoir for it near the arch of Dolabella, under the garden of the Villa Mattei, now called the Villa Cœlimontana, and from thence it passed, still underground, to the cliff of the Cœlian, opposite to the Aventine. A short tunnel was made from this deep reservoir to a Nymphæum under the Cœlian, now S. Stefano Rotondo, called of Septimius Severus. The ruins of it are shewn in 895; a *specus* has been traced from one to the other.

Appia, as the lowest (this is given in 834*, 1941*).

The Reservoirs of this most ancient and very deep aqueduct were first in the quarries before mentioned, and even in Rome were chiefly also in quarries, as at the mouth; but just within the Porta Maggiore, and close to the gardens of S. Croce, formerly the Sessorian Palace, are two large reservoirs very near together, supposed to have been the Gemelli or twin reservoirs mentioned by Frontinus, and these are so deep that they appear to have belonged to the Aqua Appia. Some excavations attempted in them in 1867 were stopped by water (410, 411, 695*). This aqueduct is believed to have entered Rome on the northern side of these gardens, and to have been first received in the reservoir afterwards called after S. Helena, which is very deep, and in this situation (546).

II. ANIO VETUS, MADE IN THE YEAR OF ROME 481, B.C. 272 [c].

The Anio Vetus and the Anio Novus are in fact branches of the river Anio, which falls into the Tiber a short distance above Rome. The water is there seen to be much more pure than that of the Tiber, and after it falls into the muddy Tiber its clear water can be distinguished for a long distance. Several of the aqueducts, as the Appia and the Virgo, are springs, that fell into that river; but part of the water was intercepted and brought into Rome, each in its own distinct *specus*. This was the case with the Anio Vetus, at a much higher level above Tivoli, but below Subiaco. The river itself may be considered to belong to the system of the Aqueducts, and the series of magnificent cascades by which it falls from

its high level, are partly artificial, are connected with them, and illustrate their history. Those in Tivoli (1545, 1546, 1547, 1548), the engineers had great difficulty in avoiding. The one near Vico - Varo (1544), above Tivoli, is near the point from which the aqueduct was taken, which is near the valley called Arsoli (1549). It can be seen in the valley of the Arches, two miles above Tivoli, at the foot of one of the piers of the Marcian Arcade (1054), and the one seems to have followed the other all the way into Rome. It passes along with it over the Ponte di S. Antonio, which is one of the finest bridges on the whole line of the Aqueducts, eight miles below Tivoli, across the valley and mountain stream called S. Antonio (1530). This aqueduct can generally be distinguished by being half-underground, or very near the surface. It was repaired or restored by Augustus and Trajan [d], and most of the remains now visible are of their time, and both the *specus* and the *castella* can generally be known by being faced with *opus reticulatum*, so much used at that time. There is a fine reservoir or *castellum* for it near Tivoli, with very peculiar work of this description, and extremely picturesque (950). Another is against a bank, and half underground, near the Torre Fiscale, three miles from Rome, and close to the foot of the Claudian Arcade (896, 1028, 1029). Remains of others may still be seen at the foot of the Wall of Rome in several places, they were distinctly visible in 1870, when these photographs were taken; but have been almost obliterated since in the *restoration* (?) of the wall by the municipal architect. One is near the Porta Metronia (983), and another

---

[c] See Frontinus de Aqueductibus, c. 6.   [d] Ibid., c. 125, and 93.

at the Porta Latina (985). Remains of other *piscinæ* are visible near the Amphitheatrum Castrense, on the rock at the foot of the wall (868, 969, 970); at this point one branch of it seems to have been brought into Rome along the line of the Via Appia Nova, which runs near the spot, and entered Rome just beyond, by the Porta Asinaria. It can also be seen at the foot of a wall by the side of the Via Labicana, near the Porta Maggiore, and readily distinguished by the usual reticulated work (1337). One branch enters Rome at the foot of the Marcian Arcade, close to the Porta Maggiore (59), and the *specus* was visible at that gate, until it was concealed by a brick wall by the modern builders. It passes through the City Wall there, and is visible on the other side in the inner road, in the wall of the garden still under the level of the Marcian Arcade (1876). Here it forked off, one branch went to the left, along the line of the wall of the garden, to a great reservoir for it at an angle close to the junction of two roads, one called the Via Labicana the other the Via di Porta Maggiore, coming from the church of S. Maria Maggiore. At this spot there is a very large and fine reservoir in several chambers at a considerable depth, corresponding to the level of the Anio Vetus; 538 is a view of it, and 700* is a section of it. From this great reservoir two small *specus* in this part appear to have gone into the *specus* of the Appia in the Cœlian, under the Arches of Nero, and are visible going into the bank on which this fine arcade stands (854).

Another important branch turns to the north upon the high bank of the Kings, on which the Wall of Aurelian

was afterwards built. There are remains of *castella* for it near the Porta S. Lorenzo (869), and further to the south near the Porta Nomentana (871), after passing the Prætorian Camp. It had previously gone under the Porta Chiusa, which was shewn in the excavation of 1868, and in the photograph 1057. The *specus* runs under the wall of the Camp all round. It is still visible on the north side, faced with the reticulated work under the fine brickwork of Tiberius (870). There was an opening into it at the north-east corner of the camp, into which a dog or a boy might be sent (981, 982), until it was closed in the recent *restoration*. Remains of it may still be seen at the foot of the wall in several places by experienced eyes. The general plan of this aqueduct is shewn in Nos. 1970*, 1971*, 1976*, 1977*, and 1967*.

III. MARCIA, MADE IN THE YEAR OF ROME, 608, B.C. 145 *.

This aqueduct was made in the year B.C. 145, and has its source a few miles below Subiaco; the springs are collected in a small lake called Aqua Serena (1537), the water from which flows into the river Anio; but a portion of it was intercepted for this aqueduct, and is now again taken from the same spot and brought into Rome. It has always been celebrated for its extreme coldness and great purity. The old *specus* or viaduct was found in 1870 in this lake, having long been concealed by being under water; but by drawing off some of the water it was brought to light, and the engineer of the new company decided on carrying his new *specus* up to this point. The previous plan had been to draw the water

---

* Frontinus de Aqueductibus, c. 6.

from another lake nearer to Rome, which is nearly equally good water, but not the real Aqua Marcia so much prized, and this is now again brought into Rome. The source of the old aqueduct is celebrated for its extremely picturesque character, as well as for the fine construction of the arcade of large square stones, and the scientific arrangement of the reservoirs (*castella aquarum*) and filtering-places (*piscinæ*). The sources in the Aqua Serena are shewn in Nos. 1538, 1539. Another source for an additional supply was on the lake of the Mole d'Agosta, 1543.

In the earlier part of its course the *specus* is underground; but on arriving at the valley called the Valley of the Arches, about two miles above Tivoli, it emerges upon the fine arches which give the name to the valley, and is here carried across the river Anio. These arches are in two series, and are among the most picturesque objects in the neighbourhood of Rome; the effect is improved by a medieval tower built upon the first pier of the bridge. This is shewn in Nos. 1053, 1054.

It then appears again on the other side of Tivoli, on the road called the Promenade of Garciano, which is on the edge of the hill looking towards Rome, and above the winding road up the hill; S. Peter's is visible from this point. On this platform there are a number of fine remains of the *specus* and of the *castella* of the Aqueducts, some of the finest of which are of the Marcia. The Plan and Section of a very fine Reservoir and Piscina here is given in No. 535[e].

Another very fine one has a wall on the edge of the cliff of the character called Cyclopean (Nos. 1513 and 1528). Chambers of this remarkable early reservoir are shewn in Nos. 1520 and 1521.

A considerable part of this aqueduct was rebuilt by Augustus[f] (B.C. 11), and again about a century afterwards by Trajan[g], and of the *specus* of that time we have examples in 1524 and 1525, shewing a very peculiar kind of the ornamental construction called *Opus Reticulatum*. Another reservoir of this time is shewn in 1526, and an earlier one belonging to the original construction of the kind called *Opus Incertum*, which probably belongs to the earlier period, is shewn in 1527.

From Tivoli the Aqueducts again pass underground for some miles, gradually winding down the hill from the high level to that of Rome on the Campagna, at about seven miles distance. They were carried upon bridges, some of which are very fine and picturesque, across the gorges of the hills and the mountain streams. At the place where they arrive at the lower ground, there are large reservoirs and filtering-places for them, and the locality is called from them the Piscinæ.

From thence they are carried on the fine and celebrated arcades across the Campagna, presenting some of the finest pictures in the neighbourhood of Rome.

At the Piscinæ, the Tepula and Julia, from the Alban Hills near Marino, were added to the Marcia, and carried on the same arcade. The greater part of them was destroyed, and used for building materials by the engineers of the Aqua Felice in the sixteenth century; but there are some very remarkable and picturesque remains of the arcade at intervals, the more interesting because so little is left of it. One fine piece remains

---

[f] Frontinus, c. 125. [g] Ibid., c. 93.

at a locality called Sette Bassi and Roma Vecchia, five miles from Rome (1435), where a small portion of each of the three Aqueducts on an arcade can be seen in Nos. 1006 and 536, and the Piscinæ near to it, 534, 1434, 1438.

This arcade is seen again at the Torre Fiscale, a medieval tower built upon the aqueducts at one of the points of junction, and at one of the angles, which they made at every half mile. Here the more lofty arcade of the Claudia and Anio Novus is carried over that of the Marcia, Tepula, and Julia ; while the Anio Vetus runs underground at the foot of it, and the Felice is built up against it ; so that at this point seven aqueducts cross each other, an'd have a tall medieval tower built on the top of them [b]. The Torre Fiscale, with this remarkable junction, is shewn in Nos. 528, 529, 530, 531, 532. A plan and section of it are given in 689*.

There is another angle and crossing at the Porta Furba, half-a-mile nearer to Rome, which makes another very picturesque point of view (shewn in Nos. 551, 552). A small portion of it remains built into a gardener's cottage at another angle, about a mile from Rome, and a fine large reservoir near to it. The ground then rises, and the arcade is buried for some distance ; the upper part of the arches of brick, as rebuilt by Trajan, are then visible by the side of the old road that runs close to the northern side of the great Claudian arcade, on the line of the Marcian, which was parallel to the Claudian for some miles into Rome.

It then occurs again very conspicuously at the last angle, close to the Porta Maggiore, where the Claudia was again carried over it, and afterwards incorporated in the City Wall of Aurelian. Here the last pier of the arcade remains with the three *specus* of the Marcia, Tepula, and Julia passing through the wall at a right angle (31, 59). Inside the wall a part of the first arch remains with the *specus* upon it (60) ; on the other side of the road, the pier of the same arch remains built into the wall of the garden ; and a little further on in the garden or vineyard, a gardener's house is made out of another reservoir or *castellum aquæ* (538 ; section, 700*).

It then passes again underground parallel to the city wall for a short distance, and near the Minerva Medica it runs into the bank on which that great wall is carried. A portion of this underground arcade was brought to light in some excavations in 1871, but is now covered up again (2320). After passing underground in the bank on which the wall stands for some distance, it emerges near the Porta Tiburtina, now called Porta di S. Lorenzo (see a plan and section of this in No. 1938*). As the ground here is lower it is on an arcade, one arch of which is made into the gate (21, 1870), and a portion of the *specus* is very distinctly visible on the southern side of the gate, with an opening into it by which persons can go inside of it (shewn in Nos. 69, 572*, and 1487).

After passing the Porta Tiburtina, it went on upon the bank or outer *mœnia* of Rome to the Prætorian Camp, and there was a large reservoir for it near the Porta Chiusa, remains of which were visible in the excavations of 1868, with the wall of Rome built across it (shewn in 1059).

---

[b] They remind English people of the Clapham Junction of the railways near London, where trains crossing each other at different levels can be seen.

From this reservoir the three aque- ducts, Marcia, Tepula, and Julia, were carried along the side of the old road to the inner gate in the great *agger* of Servius Tullius on the Viminal, where the railway station has now been made, and where the three Roman princes carried on excava- tions in 1869, in which they found the upper *specus ;* that of the Julia, which was left open for a time, pass- ing between the *cippi* or boundary- stones, with inscriptions upon them, recording that *the three aqueducts* passed there between them.

Another division of the Marcia went along the same line as the Arches of Nero to the Cœlian, and along that hill as far as the great reservoir over the arch of Dolabella ; then turning to the left or south, it came to an end above or over the Porta Capena[1]. These words may mean—either, in the reservoir on the cliff of the Cœlian Hill just *above* the gate, rebuilt in the time of Trajan, of which the remains are shewn in 1147* ;—or, in the reservoir in the valley close to the west side of that gate (also rebuilt in the time of Trajan, and now a gardener's house, as before mentioned). In that case it must have passed over the gate, and the *specus* that is cut in the wall of the western tower be- longed to it (710*).

The general plan of the Aqua Marcia near its source] is shewn in 1972*, and the line of its course in 1981*, 1982* ; the bridge for it in 1983*.

In the early part of its course, above Tivoli, the new aqueduct for this water, called the Aqua Marcia Pia, is carried on a stone *specus* upon an arcade, after the same fashion as the old one (a portion of this new arcade is shewn in No. 1553).

IV. THE TEPULA, and V. THE JULIA, being carried on the same arcade as the Marcia for the seven miles into Rome, have left remains visible in some places, especially at the Gates of Rome, the Porta Maggiore (31), and the Porta Tiburtina (21, 572*) ; in other places, they have generally been destroyed. Near the Sette Bassi, there is a portion of the *specus* of the Julia visible just at the surface of the ground, the other two being then subterranean, as the level is rather higher in this part than usual. This portion has been examined by Signor Moraldi, at a junction whence a branch was carried to supply a reservoir at the great villa called Sette Bassi, and there are remains of the loch in the channel to turn off the water, shewing the same arrangement as in a modern canal. (A plan and section of this is given in 696*.) The *specus* near this point, built of concrete faced with brick, is also shewn in 1006. The *specus* of the Marcia is always of squared stone, so that one is readily distinguished from the other. There are remains of a *castellum aquæ* or reservoir for the Tepula, near the Porta Tiburtina, or Porta Viminalis of Frontinus, now called Porta di S. Lorenzo. This is shewn in the Plan of that Gate, Nos. 1111* and 1238*, and a view of it in No. 25. It is a remarkable building of brick of the first century, and has on a level with the *specus* a series of small corbels projecting from it, evidently intended to carry a *hourd,* or wooden balcony as a passage for the Aquarii, and perhaps for defence also. It is in- corporated in the great Wall of Aure- lian. It projects slightly from the line of that wall, and the end of the *specus,* with its triangular head, is visible in the angle.

---

[1] Supra Portam Capenam, F. i. 19.

V. Julia.

Between this building and the gate, but within the wall, though on the bank on which it stands, are slight remains of another *castellum aquæ*, supposed to have been for the Julia (Nos. 26, 869, 1873), which has its external face in the direction of the wall, and must have been concealed by it when that was built. This is also of the first century, as is shewn by the brickwork, and it seems to have been a *castellum aquæ* by the disproportional size of the buttresses used to support the weight of the water, one of the invariable marks of such a structure. The other mark is the peculiar cement with which the wall is lined, called *Opus Signinum* in Latin, *Coccio Pesto* in Italian, which is made of broken pottery, and is the hardest cement that is known; it is often impossible to break it, even after it has been exposed to the weather for centuries.

A plan and section of the ground between the two gates, called by Frontinus Esquilina (S. Lorenzo) and Viminalis (Maggiore), shew the difference of level, and the three aqueducts passing underground in the middle between the two gates, and carried on arches at both ends near the gates (see No. 1938*).

The plan of the ground at the sources of the Tepula and Julia is given in 1980*.

VI. The Virgo (now called Aqua di Trevi) was made in the year of Rome 732, b.c. 21.

This aqueduct has its sources in the meadows of Lucullus, on the banks of the river Anio, on the old Via Collatia, eight miles from Rome, about a mile further than the Aqua Appia, not at the same level, but comparatively near the surface. There are several springs, each of which has its own separate reservoir just below the surface of the ground; in some of them the vault is scarcely perceived. These are also called conduit-heads (864, 863, 862). From each of these small reservoirs a conduit runs into the central reservoir (860, 861), which is considerably larger, circular in form, surrounded by a wall, lined with the cement called *coccio pesto*, and one part of this central reservoir under the road now remains. This is near Salone, with its medieval tower. (See the Plan, 1155*.)

From this large central reservoir the surplus water is carried off by short conduits into the country ditches, and so into the river Anio. The main *specus* into Rome begins at the central reservoir, and runs generally underground along the line of the old Via Collatina, now called Lunghezza. The course of the aqueduct can be clearly traced by the small pyramidal or conical structures over the wells at regular intervals, called Respirators (660*), or which might have been called Ventilators, as they give air to the *specus* below. It runs in the high bank of the old road for two or three miles, behind the ruin called Torre d' Scavi, supposed to be the Thermæ of the Gordiani, in a direct line towards the Porta Maggiore; but about half-a-mile before arriving there, it turns sharp to the north along the bank of the great *foss* or valley, and being underground is traced by the Respirators. Further to the north, beyond S. Agnes, at some little distance, the old line can be traced in the catacomb of S. Priscilla on the Via Salaria, where the *specus* is visible, half filled up with the deposit of clay (1109*, 1466). In the road on the bank on which the Wall of Aurelian is built, near the Porta Salaria, it can be traced by the low arcade at the foot of the wall which is built upon it (5).

But when the line was altered, it was carried still further to the north, and it enters Rome under the garden of the French Academy (the Villa Medici); it here is marked by two *cippi* (2088, 2089), with inscriptions upon them, and under the garden is a large reservoir very deep, level with the ground in the great foss on the outside, and with the Campus Martius inside the walls. It was then divided into two branches, one of which went along the Via de Condotti, the other along the Via del Nazzareno (83, 1108*) to the Fountain of Trevi, rebuilt in A.D. 1735 (1356); originally, it went to the north end of the Septa, near the Pantheon. Some remains of this were shewn in 1871 in the Piazza di S. Ignazio (2326). The *specus* can be seen, with an inscription upon it recording repairs by the Emperor Claudius (82), in the yard behind a house near the Palazzo del Buffalo.

The plan of the ground at the sources of the Aqua Virgo (or de Trevi), is given in 1968*, and Sections of it in 1979*.

VII. THE ALSEATINA.

This aqueduct was made by Augustus in the year of Rome 763, A.D. 10, to bring water for his great Naumachia, or sham naval battles in the Trastevere; the water was not good for drinking[k]. It was brought from the lake called Alseatina, in the hills on the western side of Rome. It is altogether distinct from the great series of aqueducts on the eastern side. The source can be seen in the bank of the lake, and the *specus* or subterranean conduit can now be entered, the water of the lake having

recently been drained, and reduced to a much lower level.

To these was added from another lake about three miles distant from the Alseatina, another branch called the Sabatina. The two conduits were united after a few miles near the old city of Cariæ, at a *castellum aquæ* or reservoir, now made into a house, and called the Osteria Nuova. The Alseatina was at the lowest level of all the aqueducts, and it is now very difficult to see any remains of it, except the *specus* in the lake at its source.

Trajan afterwards adopted the Aqua Sabatina, but omitted the Alseatina, and carried the Sabatina at the highest level instead of the lowest (see Aqua Sabatina, Aqueduct X.) Pope Paul V., who restored these aqueducts to use, went back to the Alseatina lake, and his *specus* can be seen there on a different side of the lake to that of Augustus; both are now left dry. There is, near the junction at the Osteria Nuova, a remarkable flight of steps for the use of the *aquarii*, or the men who had charge of the aqueducts. It passes through the upper *specus*, and goes down to the lower one (No. 2959*). The respirators of these two lines can be seen and traced; they are of a different size and form. The two can be seen close together at the Osteria Nuova (No. 2960*). The *specus* is also seen in No. 2961*.

VIII. THE CLAUDIA, AND
IX. THE ANIO NOVUS, A.D. 38—52.

These two aqueducts were made together, or were so closely connected that we cannot separate their history, although they were not the same water; the Anio Novus came from some miles higher up the river Anio

---

[k] See Frontinus de Aqueductibus, caps. 11, 18, 22, and 71.

than the Claudia. The latter was, like the previous aqueducts, taken from springs, that were intercepted before they fell into the river Anio ; but the Anio Novus was part of the river itself, in which a gigantic loch was made by building a great wall across it, about a hundred yards in front of a natural waterfall, and forcing the water to flow over it, forming a magnificent cascade, and at the same time causing some of the water to flow through the *specus* which was cut in the cliff by the side of the river, at a rather lower level than the top of the wall. The sources of the Claudia are below this cascade, those of the Anio Novus are above it. The line of each of these aqueducts is distinct in all the early part of its course ; but after they come down to the valley of the Campagna of Rome, at the Piscinæ, the two are carried on the same fine lofty arcade into Rome.

These were the highest, and passed over the Marcian arcade with the three aqueducts upon it. They form the finest feature in the landscape on the eastern side of Rome. The sources are above Subiaco, and in what is considered by artists as some of the most picturesque scenery in the world. The photographs illustrating this are very numerous, the subjects being some of the best that can be imagined for this purpose. The history of these two most important aqueducts can now be better seen in this series of photographs than in any other manner, and better understood than by any written description of them, after the outline of their history is once given.

They were begun in the year of Rome 789, A.D. 38, under the Emperor Caius Cæsar, or Caligula ; carried on and completed by his successor, Clau-

dius, in the year of Rome 803, A.D. 52. They were therefore fourteen years in construction, according to Frontinus[1] ; but Nero was then married to Octavia, he was the actual governor of Rome, and he carried on the great work upon what are called the Arches of Nero, along the Cœlian Hill, as far as the arch of Dolabella, where a large reservoir for this water was built. This work was afterwards carried on by his successors in three branches, one to the Colosseum, a second to the Palatine, and over it to the Capitol, and a third to the Aventine. Frontinus himself, who has left us his admirable treatise on the subject, had the direction of these works for many years ; he was Curator Aquarum under the Emperors Nerva and Trajan, and some of the greatest works were done in his time,—at his suggestion, and according to his plans.

Some of the sources of the Claudia were in the lake of S. Lucia, below Subiaco, between that and Vico Varo (see 1536). In its course through the hills the *specus* is almost entirely underground, and cannot be shewn in photographs ; but the line of its course is shewn in the map of the aqueducts from Rome to Subiaco, reduced by photography in Nos. 1967* to 1984*, especially in Nos. 1976*, 1978*, 1979*, 1981*. It crosses mountain streams on the bridges called Ponte Lupo (1532) and Ponte di S. Antonio (1530) ; and an inscription relating to it, of A.D. 88, is given in No. 1976*.

When it reaches the level ground of the Campagna, nearly on the same level as the hills of Rome, the *piscina* for it is subterranean, and only the summit of this is visible, looking like a *tumulus* only (688) ; but from this the *specus* is seen to emerge, at first only just above ground, but gra-

---

[1] Frontinus de Aqueductibus, cap. 13, 14, 18, 20.

dually getting higher (or the soil, in fact, is getting lower), until it is carried on the grand series of arches or arcades across the country, which remain nearly perfect for some miles, as far as the Sette Bassi and Roma Vecchia. In 1002, a long line of this arcade is shewn with the Claudian *specus* upon it, and the Anio Novus over that in many places; the two can readily be distinguished, by the Claudian being built of large blocks of stone (with the edges chamfered off), and the Anio Novus being faced generally with brick, occasionally with *opus reticulatum.* Nearer to Rome, this fine arcade has been very much damaged, or carried off altogether as building material by the farmers, and by the engineers of Pope Sixtus V. to build the Aqua Felice; but some portions of the old arcade remain, and are shewn in No. 1006, where the distinction between the two *specus* comes out very clearly. In 1005, two of the brick arches with which it had been strengthened by Trajan are shewn, the stone-work having all been carried away.

In 689*, a plan and section of the Torre Fiscale is shewn, with the crossing of six aqueducts. 528 is a view of this tower and of the arches of the aqueducts crossing each other under it, with the Aqua Felice in the background. 529 shews the arch of the Claudia separately, and the construction of it, with the Aqua Felice passing under this arch of the Claudia. 530 gives very distinctly the arch of the Marcia, Tepula, and Julia, with that of the Claudia passing over it. 531 and 532 are more distant and general views of that tower, and the aqueducts passing under it. 1439 is a side view of it, and of the old tombs on the Via Latina in that part. 1004 shews the arches of the Claudia and Anio Novus in perspective, and the opening into the *specus* of the

Claudia. In 550, another fine portion of the arcade is shewn, with brickwork of Trajan. The Porta Furba and a long line of the arcade is seen in the distance. 548 shews the Porta Furba at another crossing, with the fountain, and a portion of the arcade of the Felice; with the Marrana in the bed of the river Almo passing under it.

62 is a portion of the Claudian arcade, about half a mile nearer to Rome, with the arches filled up with brickwork of the time of Trajan; at this point there is another crossing. 63 shews a portion of the brickwork of Trajan, originally built to strengthen the stone arcade; but the latter has been carried away by the engineers of the Felice. 549 shews some interesting repairs of the time of Nero, with massive square buttresses faced with reticulated work. 70 is a medieval tower at the angle of the garden of the Sessorian Palace, now of the monastery of S. Croce, near the point where the aqueduct enters the wall.

547 shews the interior of the Tower and a *piscina,* at the entrance into Rome, the four chambers of which are visible, the inner wall of this tower having been destroyed; and into the interior of this the water of the Claudia entered in the first chamber and went out at the fourth. This photograph also shews the remains of a large *castellum aquæ,* now forming part of the Wall of Rome, on the north side of the garden, with a continuation of the arcade in the Wall of Rome in this part. In 544 the *specus* of the Claudia is plainly visible on the top of the wall, and remains of the Anio Novus over it. In the distance are seen some of the arches of Nero, across the valley and foss (?), from the angle near the Porta Maggiore to the Cœlian Hill. This garden might very naturally be called by Lampridius "The Garden of the

Specus," for the *specus* in the time of the Emperors must have been the most conspicuous object in it, or visible from it (542).

412 shews another of these reservoirs in the same garden, with repairs in brick by Trajan. The arcade of the Aqua Felice, built against the outside of the Wall, is also seen through the arches of the Claudia.

31. The exterior of the Porta Maggiore, with the *specus* over it, the lower one the Claudia, the upper one the Anio Novus. (The inscription of A.D. 404 is given in 1872.) Under these, but still on the top of the wall, the *specus* of the Aqua Felice may be seen, built as usual of rough stone concrete. To the right or north of this may be seen the three *specus* of the Marcia, Tepula, and Julia, passing through the wall in the opposite direction, now under the Felice, and originally under the Claudia and Anio Novus. These three *specus* are carried upon one of the piers of the Marcian arcade, built into the great wall. Just beyond these, further to the right, is part of the last tower of the Claudian arcade.

32. The Porta Maggiore, with the *specus* on it, seen sideways, and the north side of the Baker's tomb.

The last tower and *piscina* of the Aqua Claudia; it stands at an angle of the wall projecting from it, and shews clearly that it stood there when the wall was built by Aurelian, and then incorporated into it. When the fortifications of Honorius at this gate were destroyed in 1838, the inscription relating to the aqueduct was preserved and built up to the right or south of the gate (shewn in 1872). Within the wall, behind the tower,

- is a large reservoir or *castellum aquæ*, of which there are slight remains, shewn in 967 and 968.

A panoramic view of the line of the Claudian arcade, on the north side of the Sessorian gardens, taken from the extreme end of them at the west, is shewn in Nos. 542 and 543. On the left hand is the beginning of the arches of Nero, going across the foss towards the Cœlian; then the Porta Maggiore is seen sideways, with the two *specus* on the top of it. Under this is part of one of the two great reservoirs believed to have been the Gemelli of Frontinus. Then comes the western wall of the Sessorian gardens, rebuilt by S. Helena, the construction being of the time of Constantine. To the extreme right is the ruin of the Basilica or Great Hall of the Sessorian Palace, repaired by him. This is miscalled a temple of Venus and Cupid on some of the maps.

Having thus traced the Aqua Claudia from its sources into Rome, we must now do the same for

THE ANIO NOVUS,

which in its early part is distinct from it, as we have said.

1514. Sources of the Anio Novus above Subiaco. The river Anio in the highest point, with which the aqueducts are connected, is seen winding through a gorge in the rocky mountain, with remains of the bars or dams, across the river, forming the two upper lakes or lochs. The celebrated monasteries of S. Scholastica and S. Benedict are visible on the hill to the left.

1515. The River Anio, a little lower down, with remains of the second barrage or dam across it, forming the third loch or lake, with the modern bridge built upon the ruins of the old wall that formed the bar. Chapels of the monks of S. Benedict are visible on the hill to the right.

1534. The Bridge of S. Francis, over one of the branches of the Anio that meet near the rocks before mentioned, above Subiaco.

1517. Remains of a great reservoir or *castellum aquæ*, of the time of Trajan, on the bank of the lake or loch before mentioned. The wall is faced with *opus reticulatum*, with layers of brick at intervals, the usual construction of the time of Trajan.

1518. The modern bridge, far below, and remains of the old high wall on which it is built, are seen under it; below are the cliffs of the third lake or loch, cut into a circular form. In the bed of the stream are large stones fallen from the wall or bar across the river.

1519. Remains of another *castellum aquæ* above Subiaco, and the mouth of a cave connected with the aqueduct.

1555. *Specus* of the Anio Novus cut in the cliff of the valley of the Anio. This is below the level of the great bar, and the water was forced to go through the *specus* into Rome by the bar being higher than the *specus*. A modern winding road has now been cut here, and the rock has been in part cut away, shewing an opening into the *specus*, which is six feet high and two feet wide. Above is seen a tower and an embattled wall of the modern Villa Gori.

1516. Part of the *specus* of Trajan, who repaired this aqueduct. The *specus* is cut as a tunnel in the cliff, with a reservoir by the side of it.

1556. A view of the gorge in the mountains above Subiaco, where the three lakes are situated.

1536. A small lake at the source of the spring called Fons Novus Antoninianus, one of the sources of the Anio Novus.

1558. Cascade at the Paper Mill, on the site of a *piscina* of the Anio Novus, above Subiaco.

1057. Arches of the bridges of the Marcia and Anio Novus, in the Valley of the Arches above Tivoli.

1052. Arch of the bridge on the Anio Novus, in the Valley of the Arches above Tivoli, with a medieval tower

built upon it, forming one of the most picturesque objects in the neighbourhood of Rome.

1522. Specus of the Anio Novus below Tivoli, on the road to Garciano, called the Promenade, with openings into it, and an old tomb in front of it. This promenade is through an olive wood, and the roots of the olive trees run into many of the ruins.

1523. One side of a *castellum aquæ* of the aqueduct above the road to Garciano, faced with *opus reticulatum*.

1529. A bridge across a valley that passes the road to Garciano. This bridge is above the road on the left, in the valley called the Arcinelli.

1531. Ponte de S. Antonio, a fine bridge for the aqueduct below Tivoli, across a gorge. It is seen from above looking down upon it, with the chapel of S. Antony at the end of it, and a medieval castle in the distance. The road for horses, and the remains of the *specus* by the side of it, are here visible.

1532. Ponte Lupo, near Poli, west side, below Tivoli, the finest of all the bridges of the aqueducts. It crosses a valley from one cliff to the other, and is a solid wall for part of the way, the rest on arches. The two *specus* are here visible, as seen from below on the west side.

687. Arrived in the valley of the Campagna, the great *piscina* of the Anio Novus and that of the Claudia, which is near to it, is underground, and the summit of it only is visible, appearing like a tumulus. It is near the old Via Latina, and below the present roads to Albano, Frascati and Marino.

74 and 75. After leaving the great *piscinæ*, the two *specus* are carried on the fine arcade, of which a panoramic view is here given, shewing its general effect for some miles.

554. Passing by the remains of Roma Vecchia to the Torre Fiscale and the Porta Furba (given under the head

of the Aqua Claudia), the *specus* rises to a remarkable reservoir, which from its great elevation must have belonged to the highest of the aqueducts. It is a most picturesque one, near the Mausoleum of S. Helena, but is earlier than her time; it belongs rather to that of Trajan, being faced with fine reticulated work, with layers of bricks on the exterior. The interior is distinguished by remarkably solid central buttresses, to support the wall against the pressure of the water (553).

926. Another large reservoir of the same period and style, and at nearly the same level; it occurs about a mile further from the main line of the aqueducts, at the place called Torre de' Scavi, where the Thermæ of the Gordiani were afterwards made. This appears also to have belonged to the Anio Novus, as no other aqueduct is high enough for the water to have reached it.

ARCHES OF NERO.

At the great reservoir inside the Porta Maggiore (the Porta Esquilina of Frontinus), the water of the Claudia and the Anio Novus was united for the general use of the City. This aqueduct entered on the highest ground in Rome, and the water supplied the deficiencies of any of the other aqueducts in case of need. Being a part of the river Anio, it never failed. It was forced to come through Rome, as has been shewn by the arrangements in the bed of the Anio above Subiaco. This united water was carried to all the fourteen Regiones of Rome, and in order to ensure an abundant supply, it was conveyed in the great stone *specus*, on the fine arches of Nero along the whole length of the Cœlian Hill for more than a mile; at the west end of the Cœlian an enormous reservoir was built for it on the level of the *specus* at the top of these arches,

so that the base of the reservoir was fifty feet from the ground, and the road passed under it. From this great central reservoir, at a very high level, the water was distributed in various directions.

Before arriving at the Cœlian Hill, it had to be conveyed to and along the Cœliolum (now the Lateran Hill). It had come through the gardens of the Sessorium, as we have seen, in the two separate *specus*, after it had entered Rome at the extreme eastern corner, on the north side of these gardens, which are nearly half a mile long. These are *the palace gardens* mentioned by Frontinus. The Sessorium with its gardens (now the monastery of S. Croce in Gerusalemme) had been one of the two Prætorian camps, this one being at the south end of the great *agger* of the Tarquins, which formed the outer *mœnia* of Rome on the eastern side. The one, called the Prætorian Camp, is at the north end of the same great bank.

Each of these fortified camps was surrounded by a great wide and deep foss or trench. These great banks and trenches are usually mistaken for natural hills and valleys; but natural hills and valleys are not merely high banks fifty feet high and perhaps a hundred feet wide, nor are natural valleys long narrow trenches of the same dimensions, running on each side of the great banks, being in fact the trenches from which the earth has been thrown to form the banks. Such a bank with such trenches can be clearly traced all round Rome by eyes that are accustomed to examine such things, although modern buildings have disguised them so much that an ordinary observer does not see them. People cannot see over modern walls of twelve feet high, still less over the great Wall of Aurelian fifty feet high, and they do not think of comparing the level of the ground on each side of that wall, nor can they easily do so. These great ancient earthworks were extremely convenient for the engineers of the Aqueducts, which were brought upon the high banks at the farthest corner. They were carried along the bank on the north side of the Sessorium, from its north-east corner to the south-west angle, where the great bank of the Tarquins joins on to it. Some branches of the Aqueducts, perhaps the main stream in some cases, were then carried along this high bank of the Tarquins to the north, as far as the other Prætorian Camp, and beyond it along the outer wall of Rome, as we have seen in the case of the Anio Vetus, the Marcia, Tepula, and Julia. These did not pass through the Sessorium, but parallel to it about a hundred yards on the north of it. The Claudian arcade had been at about that distance on the north of it, all the way from the Piscinæ into Rome. The Marcian arcade was made nearly over the Anio Vetus, which ran between that arcade and the Claudian, but much nearer to the Marcian.

On entering Rome, this main stream went straight on through the great bank to the large reservoir on the inner side. The reservoirs for the Tepula and Julia were much to the north, near the Porta di S. Lorenzo (the Porta Viminalis of Frontinus), as we have seen ; that of the Marcia was much closer to the Porta Esquilina. The two great reservoirs, called by Frontinus the Gemelli, were made in the great foss between the Sessorium (S. Croce) and the Cœliolum (the Lateran). They had probably been originally made for the Aqua Appia and the Anio Vetus, being both at a low level, though one was much deeper than the other. Advantage was taken of these ancient reservoirs to erect the higher

one required for the reception of the waters of the Claudia and Anio Novus over it, or by the side of it, as was very usual throughout Rome. The later reservoirs are always made nearly over the old ones. This is equally the case here at the entrance into Rome and at the other end of the Cœlian. The great high reservoir of Nero is close by the side of, and really over, the great subterranean reservoir of the Aqua Appia (now under the garden of the Villa Cœlimontiana, as described in the account of the Appia).

The foregoing explanation seems necessary to explain the photographs that now follow, belonging to the Arches of Nero. The first of these (No. 77) shews the junction with the Porta Maggiore ; the two *specus* that pass over that great gate are visible to the right of the photograph. The beginning of the Arches of Nero is then seen, where they have to cross the great wide and deep foss of the Sessorium, and were therefore strengthened by sub-arches, as seen in No. 76. A more close view of these arches, nearly at the same point, is seen in 66.

These arches were used by the engineers of the Aqua Felice whenever they suited their purpose, and cut about or destroyed without mercy ; they also made use of an old *specus* to carry their metal pipes whenever it was convenient to do so, and the *old specus* that ran along the Cœlian was very convenient for that purpose. 1295* is from a drawing made to shew this. The *specus* of the Aqua Felice was first carried on the lower arches of the double arcade of Nero, the upper part of the arcade being destroyed. The metal pipes were then carried down into the old subterranean *specus* (*the Specus Vetus* of Frontinus). This is in the same garden or vineyard as the Gemelli, in the great foss between the Sessorium and the end of one of the banks of the Tarquins, (on which the garden of the Villa Volkonski has been made, and along which the Arches of Nero run.) A portion of the grand arcade, with the *specus* very visible on the top of it, is shewn in 759. This is close to the Scala Santa of the Lateran; the arcade carrying the aqueduct passed along the bank on the north side of the Lateran fortress on the Cœliolum, and supplied that with water.

On the western side of the Lateran fortress is another great foss, between the Cœliolum and the east end of the Cœlian Hill. It was either thought more convenient to make a bank across that great foss for the aqueduct to rest upon, or this bank which traverses that great foss had been made before for an upper road, and was used first for the Aqua Appia and the Anio Vetus, and afterwards by Nero. The existence of such a foss between the east end of the Cœlian Hill and the Cœliolum is denied by those who have not paid attention to the subject, and have not been into the gardens and vineyards to examine it; but the fact is a matter of demonstration. The tomb of the first century (miscalled the House of Verus, probably a tomb of the great Lateran family), being on the western bank of that fortress and the eastern bank of the foss, and the other tomb of the first century also, in the garden of what was the Museum of Campana (*under* an arch that carries the modern road), on the western side of that great foss, are a demonstration that there was such a foss on the east side of the City of Servius Tullius, i.e. that the Cœliolum and Lateran did not form part of the City at that time. (See my chapter on the Tombs, and the photographs of these two tombs, 174 and 1942).

The Arches of Nero remain on the Cœlian in many parts of the line, by the side of the road from the Lateran to S. Stefano Rotondo and the Navicella, with the arch of Dolabella, which was under the great reservoir of Nero, and formed the entrance of the Claudium. The Arches of Nero are faced with the finest brickwork in the world (ten bricks to the foot, as usual at that period, and are chosen as typical examples). This is well shewn in 78, and the internal construction of rubble, faced only with the fine brickwork, in 358. A line of these, shewing the picturesque effect, is shewn in 131 and 357. The aqueduct formed one of the usual angles between the Lateran and the arch at the west end of the Cœlian. It has been destroyed in this part; but this accounts for the arches being sometimes on one side of the road and sometimes on the other.

We have now arrived at the arch of Dolabella, built when he was consul, A.D. 10, as an entrance to that part of the Cœlian Hill which had been the keep when it was a separate fortress, and was afterwards made the Claudium. This arch is of very simple construction, of travertine, the same construction as the early part of the Basilica Julia, built by Julius Cæsar and Augustus. It was used by the engineers of Nero as a foundation for their great reservoir, or rather for one corner of it, as we clearly see in 72. The work of the time of Nero terminated here, but the design was carried on by his immediate successors. The water was then divided into three branches; the one on the right hand, to the north, went to the great reservoir between the Cœlian and the Esquiline, called the *Stagna Neronis*, and was used for the sham naval battles. Around these Stagna the Colosseum was afterwards built. A portion of the arcade on which the *specus* was carried is visible in the garden of the monks called the Passionists of SS. John and Paul, and is well shewn in No. 1773, looking towards the east, with the ruins of the reservoir over the arch of Dolabella, and the church of S. Stefano Rotondo in the distance. There are remains of a reservoir for this, of the third century, in the garden of the monks on the terrace of the Claudium, opposite to the Palatine, shewn in No. 1765. The ruins of the fine arcade of the Claudium stand on this terrace; the *specus* also is in a wall here, behind the arcade. A portion of another reservoir or *piscina* for them can be seen at the foot of the cliff of the Claudium, at its north-east corner, opposite that part of the Colosseum near the Meta Sudans; this is also shewn in No. 1743, with *opus reticulatum* of the time of Nero. This branch continued in use in the third century; for there are remains of another reservoir for it, again at the foot of the Claudium opposite to the Colosseum, but more to the east, near the north-east corner of the Claudium, and near to the eastern end of the Colosseum. The remains of this reservoir are shewn in No. 1735. A colonnade carrying the *specus* from this reservoir to the second story of the Colosseum, is shewn on one of the coins of Septimius Severus, who probably built this reservoir. In the corridors of the Colosseum are open stone troughs lined with the cement for water. These carried water from this aqueduct in a constant running stream to cool the air. They are work of the third century, with old inscriptions on some of them, shewing that they were made of old materials.

Another branch from the great reservoir went straight across to the Palatine, and from thence to the Capitol; it first follows the line of the road down the Clivus Scauri, on the left or southern side, and a fragment of it is visible opposite to the church of SS. John and Paul, as seen in No. 305. At the foot of the Clivus Scauri it formed an angle, and passed against the cliff on which the apse of the church was afterwards built; it now forms the lowest and last of the series of arches that are carried across the road to support the side of the church. Then, after this angle to the north, it resumes its course to the west upon the arches across the valley to the Palatine, which was a double arcade; but the lowest tier of it only remains, as is shewn in 116. A portion of the upper tier is also visible at the end of it; an arch of this upper tier remains, which, having been made into a back gate of the Palatine, has been suffered to remain, and is shewn in No. 72. A large reservoir for it was made at the south-west corner of the Palatine, on which the palace of Commodus was afterwards built; part of this reservoir and *specus* is shewn in 683 (made from a drawing). The *specus* went across the middle of the Palatine, and has been found more than once in some of the recent excavations, but not understood. It was then carried on the bridge of Caligula to the Capitol, a small portion of which remains connected with his palace, as is shewn in Nos. 1447 and 1451.

The third branch from the great reservoir over the arch of Dolabella on the Cœlian was made in the time of Trajan, to carry water to supply the thermæ on the Aventine, called after Sura, the cousin of the Emperor; these thermæ were closely connected with the private house of his family, rebuilt in his time, and called in the Regionary Catalogue "Privata Trajani," of which there are considerable remains, now subterranean. The first place where this branch of the aqueduct is visible is in another reservoir(1147)against the cliff of the Cœlian, opposite to S. Balbina. This is partly above the level of the hill, and has been thought part of the Palace of Commodus, on the Cœlian (which may possibly have been built over it, but the existing remains are of the time of Trajan). The lower part is under this, and is excavated in the cliff. These were brought to light in the excavations of A.D. 1868 (559, 1008, 1009, 1010, 1011). The plan and section of it are to be seen in 1150*, 692*. Against the cliff the aqueduct formed one of the usual angles towards the north, and this was carried across the valley on the *agger* or bank of Servius Tullius, first passing over the arch of the gate of the Porta Capena, above the Aqua Appia, on a much higher level, and on an arcade, probably a double arcade, like the Arches of Nero near the Porta Maggiore, on account of the great height at which the water had to be carried from one hill to the other. All that remains of this lofty arcade is a line of brick piers passing across from the Cœlian to the Aventine, over the Aqua Appia, before described, and passing by the north end of the Piscina Publica, as re-built in the time of Trajan over the old one, which had belonged to the older aqueducts. There are consider-able remains of the walls of this period, that divided the chambers shewn in 557, 558, 1288.

This arcade can then be traced against the cliff of the Pseudo-Aventine, on the north side of S. Balbina, though partly concealed by the fill-ing up of the space against the cliff before mentioned. The tall arcade then crosses the valley from the Pseudo-Aventine to the other part of the Aventine, and from the garden of S. Balbina to that of S. Prisca, and, in the latter garden,

there are considerable remains of it on the cliff opposite to the Palatine. At the north end is the *specus* upon the arcade (the top is open, and there is a walk upon it), 79. A small portion of the Thermæ of Sura is also shewn, with the *specus* in front of the ancient wall of tufa, called the Wall of the Latins (833).

From the *piscina* and reservoir on the cliff of the Cœlian another branch went to the south, over the spring of the Camenæ (?) 692, and near that of Egeria (?); it was carried over the Porta Metronia, and on the bank of the City Wall as far as the Porta Latina.

Another fine arcade of the time of Nero (No. 1317) leads to the Nymphæum before mentioned, where the Trophies of Marius were hung. The elevation shews that this water must have come from the highest of the aqueducts, the Anio Novus; and the remains of the reservoir near the Porta di S. Lorenzo, supposed to have been for the Aqua Julia, being on high ground, may have been for this branch, which conveyed water to the Thermæ of Titus.

X. SABATINA TRAJANA.

Great works for the aqueducts were carried on in the time of Trajan. One great work of his time was to bring water from the lake Sabatina to the top of the Janiculum. Augus-tus had previously brought water from that lake, supplementary to his aqueduct, from the lake Alseatina (VII.), to supply his Naumachia in the Trastevere; but the Aqueduct of Augustus was on the lowest level, that of Trajan on the highest. It does not appear that Trajan made use of the old *specus* of Augustus; but his aqueduct was afterwards made use of by the engineers of Pope Paul V. for the Aqua Paola, although they also brought a branch to it from the Alseatina, as Augustus had done.

That of Trajan is chiefly subterranean, and has been described under the head of the Alseatina (VII.), but nearer Rome it is above ground, and is carried on an arcade against the wall of the Villa Pamphili - Doria, near the Porta di S. Pancratio. Both the arcade and the *specus* are faced with the *opus reticulatum* of that period. (664* is from a drawing, 1065 from nature.) In some parts, one side of the *specus* has been cut away (1063). Just on the outside of that garden a large *castellum aquæ* of this aqueduct has been made into a farm-house, and in the yard of that house a branch from it can be seen (665*), apparently for the purpose of irrigation ; or, as some think, this was formerly the point of division, one branch going· to the Vatican, the other to the great fountain on the Janiculum (960), above S. Pietro in Montorio. The division now takes place at a short distance from this point. Procopius, writing in the sixth century, admires the enormous quantity of water brought by this aqueduct to the highest point in Rome ; as it descends the hill, it turns the wheels of the flour-mills. After it arrived at the low level of the ground in the Trastevere, the respirators of the pipes for this aqueduct are carried in tall pyramids resembling chimneys (540). Part of the arcade and *specus* rebuilt by Paul V., near the garden before mentioned, is shewn in 1064, with the inscription of A. D. 1609 above it.

XI. HADRIANA (?), TRAJANA (?) OR ALEXANDRINA (?).

The next great work of the period of Trajan or of Hadrian, on the eastern side of Rome, was probably begun in the time of Trajan. It brought water from springs under Labicum, now La Colonna, the same that is now brought for the Aqua Felice. The watèr from several springs was collected in a central reservoir, on which an inscription of Hadrian was found by E. Q. Visconti in the eighteenth century. This is between Pantana and Gabii, in the valley under La Colonna (1540). There are several other reservoirs of the time of Trajan or Hadrian along the line (1637, 1638). This aqueduct was considered by Fabretti to be of the time of Alexander Severus, and since his time it has usually been called the Aqua Alexandrina. It may have been partly rebuilt and brought into use again in his time, after having been choked up with stalactite, one of the springs used proving to be a petrifying spring.

Near the sources this arcade is low and much damaged, and the *specus* where it remains is nearly filled up with stalactite (1541, 1542). In some parts of the line the stalactite has all the appearance of a petrified cascade, and is evidently formed by the water oozing out and dripping and petrifying as it fell (1436). Further on there is a fine arcade for it across the country in the direction of Cento-Celle ; and in some places the arcade is double to raise the *specus* to the necessary level, as in the Arches of Nero (1428, 1429). A portion of the arcade, where it is broken off, is seen in 1427, with the tower of Cento-Celle in the distance. Another portion of this fine arcade is shewn in 1640. It is of two periods ; the upper part is of the third century, and may have been rebuilt by Alexander Severus (as has been said). At Cento-Celle the ground is high, and the aqueduct passes underground for some distance, along the side of the road towards Rome.

About a mile nearer to Rome, there is a branch aqueduct from the foot of the Marcian arcade, in the direction of the Mausoleum of S. Helena, which Fabretti considers as part of the same aqueduct; but it is difficult to see upon what grounds. There is a fine arcade here also for about a quarter of a mile; but it is of the time of Constantine, and I have not been able to trace any connection between this and the other. This arcade has been originally double, and the lower one only now remains, with a modern *specus* made upon it (555 and 556); but the water now flows *from* the Marrana, at the foot of the arcade of the great aqueducts, which were here on higher ground, and *runs down* upon this arcade to the garden and small monastery of S. Peter and Marcellinus, at the Mausoleum of S. Helena, called the Torre Pignattara, from the earthenware pots of which the vault was made.

XII. AURELIA, A.D. 185, AND XIII. SEVERIANA, A.D. 190.

These two aqueducts were made to convey water to the Thermæ of Commodus and Severus in Regio I., of which the remains were found in the excavations of 1870, just within the Porta Latina. The first part was originally made by Marcus Aurelius, for the use of his great villa on the Via Appia, called the Villa dei Quintilii, and the great reservoir and thermæ connected with it remain (2346, 2349, 2350, 2351, 2352). From thence it was brought into Rome by his successor, Ælius Aurelius Commodus. The water came from the Alban hills, near Marino (2358, 2359, 2360, 2361, 2362, 2363), at first underground, and then on an arcade, of which there are considerable remains near the Torre di Mezza Via di Albano (1626 and 1627).

From the Villa dei Quintilii it went parallel to the Via Appia. One of the reservoirs of it nearer to Rome is made into a farm-house, with a tower to it, and has the appearance of a church at a little distance; it is called the Casale di S. Maria Nuova (2348); it then passed again underground. Near the head of the valley of the Caffarella there remains a *piscina* for it nearly perfect (1372); this is very near also to the Circus of Maxentius and his son Romulus. There is another *piscina* or small reservoir for it near the church of S. Urbano, often mistaken for a tomb; here it again forms an angle, and the *specus* descends (plan and drawing, 831*) to the Nymphæum, or so-called Fountain of Egeria (262). The *specus* is then continued in the cliff of the valley of the Caffarella, from that fountain towards the tomb of the first century called Dio Ridicolo. Nearly opposite to that tomb the *specus* is visible in the cliff, with large openings into it, between which it passes underground. Wherever it was above ground it has been carried off as building materials and destroyed, so that it has not again been found until it arrives at the remains of a *piscina*, just to the south of the Porta Latina (984). It then entered the city of Aurelian through the bank on which his wall is built, and supplied the Thermæ of Commodus within that gate (as has been said), 1485, 1486.

XIV. ANTONINIANA, A.D. 215.

This aqueduct was used to supply the great Thermæ of the Antonines, now called after Antoninus Caracalla. It is more easily traced backwards, passing along the inner side of the bank on which the Wall of Aurelian is built, then upon an arcade which has been destroyed in this part, but of which remains are visible inside of the Porta Ardeatina (986), by the side of the Arch of Drusus, just within the Porta di S. Sebastiano (73, 1772, 1202). It then passes underground through the bank, and emerges in the city wall at the angle between the Porta di S. Sebastiano and the Porta Latina (539, 883). It here crosses the road, and is visible in the garden on the opposite side (884).

XV. ALEXANDRINA, A: D. 225.

The Aqua Alexandrina is mentioned by Lampridius in his life of Alexander Severus, but it was probably a branch from the Anio Novus only, as the Nymphæum engraved on one of his coins ᵐ has been identified with the ruins near S. Maria Maggiore (2126, 2127). This stands on very high ground, and the only aqueduct that could reach it was that of the Anio Novus. This branch can be traced in the wall by the piers of the arcade, which have been built into the Wall of Aurelian near the Porta Maggiore (80 A, B). The *specus* and the arches were destroyed by the engineers of the Aqua Felice ; the piers only remain, and these cease just before we arrive at the point where the railway now enters Rome through the wall (99). They come to an end directly in a line with a large reservoir, now a gardener's house, near the Minerva Medica, almost between that and the wall, but a little to the south of it ; one pier, however, of the tall arcade of the third century remains, as a sort of buttress, against that side of the fine building of the same period called the Temple of Minerva Medica (537). There are great remains of thermæ and fountains in the large vineyard in which this building stands. Some of these are of an earlier period ; but

a considerable part of them are of the third century, and of the time of Alexander Severus. The Nymphæum before mentioned was at the north end, and is a fine picturesque ruin, with very evident remains of the aqueduct in it (61, 963, 964). The water was here divided into several branches, of which we see portions of the *specus* going in different directions. One of the most important of these goes to the great reservoir of the Thermæ of Titus and Trajan, called the Sette Sale. This was made long before the time of Alexander Severus, who only rebuilt the Nymphæum ; and there is an arcade of the first century leading to this Nymphæum from a reservoir near the Porta di S. Lorenzo.

At a short distance to the south of this celebrated Nymphæum is another very curious reservoir, now in a very bad state, having been turned into a gardener's house, but which must have been of considerable importance, and probably belonged to the thermæ of the third century (2322, 2323). There is a *cippus* with an inscription, which indicates that the building was a *castellum aquæ* (2324).

XVI. ALGENTIANA, A.D. 300.

This aqueduct was made to supply the great Thermæ of Diocletian on the Viminal Hill, but is believed to have been entirely subterranean, so that little is known about it. There was a reservoir for it on the eastern side of the Thermæ, under the present railway station. Drawings and a plan of this were preserved by Visconti ᵃ.

ᵐ Cohen. Méd. Imp. Alex. Sev., (Nos. 239, 334).

ᵃ This water is not mentioned in the Regionary Catalogue, and its whole history appears doubtful. Some think

the name is a corruption of Argentina, the short stream that rises in the Lupercal or Wolf's Cave, under the northwest corner of the Palatine, as before mentioned.

XVII. THE AQUA CRABRA, THE MARRANA, A.D. 1124, AND THE RIVER ALMO.

These three may all be treated as one aqueduct for the supply of Rome, partly natural and partly artificial. They all come from the Alban Hills; the first from near Rocca di Papa on very high ground, the second from about a mile above the small and very picturesque town of Marino; the third lower down the same hill. They are all mountain streams, and partake of the usual character of such streams; in dry weather the springs that supply the Almo bring so little water, that it is only sufficient to fill some ponds for cattle at the foot of the hill. The deep bed of the river, which winds about the Campagna for miles, is therefore dry for a great part of the year, but the other two streams never fail; they are united at the foot of the hill, not far from the place where the Aqua Aurelia came from. The greater part of their united waters runs into the river Anio, but a portion of it is diverted near the ruins of the ancient fortified village or *pagus*, called *Centroni* (2315, 2316, 2317, 2318, 2319), on the road to Tusculum, (now Frascati,) about eight miles from Rome. This branch to supply Rome is first brought through an ancient tunnel of the Aqua Julia, at each end of which remains can be seen of the stone *specus* and the flood-gates (2310, 2311, 2312, 2313). The water is then conveyed in a bank of clay for about a mile, and then in the bed of one of the many branches of the mountain stream called the river Almo, and so brought into Rome (1309, 1318), under the Porta Metronia, which is built upon a bridge over it. The stream passes under some other bridges with mills upon them, and eventually falls into the Tiber through an aperture left for it in the Pulchrum Littus, or fine tufa wall of the Kings (drawing, 1235*; plans, 368*, 1234*; views, 77, 166, 157).

Another branch from it is carried from the junction or separation between the Torre Fiscale and Roma Vecchia (1937*) by the side of the cross road from the Via Appia Nova to the Via Appia Antiqua. Sometimes in the bed of the Almo, and in other parts, where the ground is low and the stream is liable to floods, an artificial canal is made for it, which may be seen in the valley of the Caffarella. This excellent plan was carried out in the most economical but effectual manner by a company in the twelfth century. This is really an aqueduct, though not usually so called; it is kept in repair by the present Water-Company, and is of great importance for Rome; as the floods to which the Almo was always liable along its whole line, and within the walls of Rome, (as is mentioned by Cicero,) are effectually kept out of Rome, and a constant, regular supply of water is obtained.

XVIII. AQUA FELICE, made A.D. 1587 by Pope Sixtus V. (Felice Peretti).

The sources of it are the springs under the hill on which La Colonna stands. The same water had been used long before, and brought into Rome by the aqueduct (XI.) of Hadrian and Trajan before mentioned. The large reservoir for the water now in use is very near to the remains of the old one of Hadrian. The construction of this aqueduct is very rude and rough, of concrete and rubble-stone only, and this stone consists entirely of old materials; still the large scale of the work, and the height at which the *specus* is carried upon the arcade, give it a grand effect. At a little distance, the inferior construction is not seen, and this almost modern aqueduct is frequently mistaken by strangers for one of the old ones of the time of the Empire, of which it is only an imitation. It is seen in several of the views of the older aqueducts in the Campagna, especially those at the Torre Fiscale (531, 1028, 1029) and the Porta Furba (68, 1437). Here it crosses the road to Frascati on an arch, with an inscription upon it. In the latter part of its course it is made on the piers of the Claudian arcade, and it enters Rome at the same point, the north-east corner of the gardens of S. Croce. After passing along the north side of them, it is divided into different branches by a reservoir at the angle, close to the south side of the Porta Maggiore (30). The principal stream then passes along upon the Wall of Aurelian (80 A, B, 81), on the same high bank as the earlier aqueducts had done ; it was cut through in making the railway, but a new bridge over that road was built for it (29). Near this it can be seen that it is carried on the piers of an older aqueduct for some distance (28). See Alexandrina (XV.) Further on towards the Porta di S. Lorenzo the ground is higher, and in order to keep the level necessary for the *specus*, it is brought within the wall, and built up against the inside of it (1871). The Marcia, Tepula, and Julia, over which it is carried, as is seen at the two gates where their arcade is visible *under* the *specus* of the Aqua Felice, are here still under it, but *underground* also, owing to

the higher level of the ground. It passes over the Porta di S. Lorenzo to a reservoir on the north side of it, and then turns to the west by the side of the road, which it crosses upon an arch, with an inscription upon it, at a short distance within that gate (81). The principal termination of it is at the Fountain of the Termini (called of Moses,) 71. Behind the fountain is a reservoir after the old fashion, which is illustrated by a plan and section (704*). The celebrated Fountain of the Triton (1196), in the Piazza Barberini, is also supplied by this aqueduct, as well as all the upper terraces upon the hills. The lower range, on the Campus Martius, is chiefly supplied by the Virgo. Another branch goes from the reservoir at the Porta Maggiore along the bank on which the Arches of Nero are carried, to the Lateran, where the fountains are supplied by this water. The old aqueduct was used according to the custom of the time, and there is a cascade *specus* from the level of the Marcia to that of the Appia (shewn in 541).

The *specus* of each of these old aqueducts was used to carry the metal pipes of the Aqua Felice, when it was convenient to do so (1295*), as has been previously mentioned.

THE AQUA MARCIA PIA was made by a Company between 1860 and 1870, and has been mentioned under the head of the Marcia (a part of it is shewn in 1553).

THE EGYPTIAN OBELISKS.

PREFACE.

THIS concise account of the Egyptian Obelisks in Rome is drawn up entirely from the inscriptions upon them. Those of the Popes, record when each was placed in its present situation. Those of the Emperors, state on what occasion each was brought to Rome. The hieroglyphics give the original history of each in Egypt. One of them only was made for the Romans, or is of their time; the others are much older, and belong to the history of Egypt, as will be seen in reading the account of them. These were brought to Rome as trophies of conquest only, and were erected in the most public places to commemorate the triumph of the Roman arms.

These hieroglyphic inscriptions have been kindly translated for me by an eminent Egyptian scholar residing in Rome during the winter, who declines to have his name published; but I am permitted to state that the translation has been compared by Dr. Birch, of the British Museum, and Dr. Bonomi, of the Soane Museum, and they agree that it is done in an accurate and careful manner. Their names will be a guarantee to the public that this portion of the work can be fully depended on.

HISTORICAL PHOTOGRAPHS ILLUSTRATIVE OF
THE EGYPTIAN OBELISKS IN ROME.

[*'he numbers refer to Mr. Parker's Catalogue.*]

I. This obelisk was originally set up by Pope Maire or Mœris, *c.* B.C. 2000 ; erected by Augustus in the Campus Martius, in front of his mausoleum ; now in the Piazza di Monte Citorio, where it was placed by Pius VI., A.D. 1792 ; this has been taken on three sides, in order that the hieroglyphics may be legible for Egyptian scholars. 1448, 1449, 1450

II. The obelisk now behind S. Maria Maggiore, was brought to Rome by Augustus, A.D. 10. It was one of the two of Pope Maire or Mœris, *c.* B.C. 2000, and was set up here by Sixtus V., A.D. 1587.

III. The obelisk now at the Lateran was originally set up by Thothmes III., *c.* B.C. 1650 ; brought to Rome by Constantine, and was put in its present place by Sixtus V., *c.* A.D. 1588. 760, 1342

IV. The obelisk in the Piazza del Popolo bears the names of Rameses II. and his father, Seti, in B.C. 1487. It was brought to Rome by Augustus, B.C. 10, and was originally placed on the Spina of the Circus Maximus. It was set up in its present situation under Sixtus V., *c.* A.D. 1590. 766, 1119, 1351

V. The obelisk at the Trinita de Monti was originally erected by Rameses II., *c.* B.C. 1450 ; it was set up in its present place by Pius VI., A.D. 1789. 649

VI. The obelisk at the Pantheon was also erected originally by Rameses II., *c.* B.C. 1450. It was placed on the Spina of the Circus Maximus, from which it was removed by Paul V., A.D. 1620, to the Piazza di S. Martino ; and was erected in its present place by Clement XI., A.D. 1711 ; it is now placed in the middle of the basin of a fountain, in front of the Pantheon. 767, 1350

VII. The obelisk now in the garden of the Villa Mattei or Cœlimontana, is another of those originally erected by Rameses II. It was erected on its present site by Sixtus V., *c.* A.D. 1590.

VIII. The obelisk now at the Vatican, in front of S. Peter's, was originally set up by Menephthah, the son of Rameses II., *c.* B.C. 1400 ; and was brought to Rome by Caligula, A.D. 40, and has an inscription of his time dedicating it to the God Augustus. It is now surmounted by a Cross ; it was placed where it now stands under Sixtus V., *c.* A.D. 1590.

IX. The obelisk which formerly stood in front of the Church of S. Lorenzo in Lucina, was originally erected by Psammeticus II., B C. 590, and was brought to Rome by Augustus, B.C. 30, and used for a sun-dial.

X. The small obelisk set up by Bernini, A.D. 1667, on the back of an elephant, in the Piazza della Minerva, has upon it the cartouche of Apries, or Pharaoh-Hophra, *c.* B.C. 570. 648

XI. The obelisk now in the Piazza Navona, was cut in Egypt for the Emperor Domitian, *c.* A.D. 90, and inscribed with his name. It was placed on the Spina of the Circus of Maxentius, and was erected in its present situation by Bernini, A.D. 1651. 1302, 1303, 1304

THE ARCHÆOLOGY OF ROME.

I. PRIMITIVE FORTIFICATIONS. Earthworks. The Seven Fortified Hills connected by Aggeres into one City.

II. WALLS AND GATES OF ROME. The XXXVII. Gates of Pliny (c. A.D. 50); Wall and Towers of Aurelian (A.D. 275): Gateway Fortresses of Honorius (A.D. 403); and Theodoric (A.D. 520); Repairs of the Popes.

III. HISTORICAL CONSTRUCTION OF WALLS (Vitruvius),—Kings,—Republic,—Empire,—Medieval.

IV. AQUEDUCTS. The IX. Aqueducts of Frontinus (A.D. 100). Later Aqueducts—Almo, Aqua Crabra, Marrana.

V. THE EGYPTIAN OBELISKS : their Inscriptions, &c.

VI. TOMBS IN AND NEAR ROME. Within the Walls, and on the Via Appia, Via Latina, &c.

VII. THE CATACOMBS. Chronology. Topography. Inscriptions. Fresco-paintings. Churches outside the Walls connected with the Catacombs.

VIII. HOUSES AND GARDENS. In the Pomœria, on the Collis Hortorum, &c. Medieval Castles and Towers.

IX. CHURCH AND ALTAR DECORATIONS. The Cosmati Family : their Ambones, Screens, Pavements (called *Opus Alexandrinum*), &c.

X. MOSAIC PICTURES IN THE CHURCHES, in Chronological Order. Early Empire,—and Christian, (Centuries Four to Sixteen),—and Frescoes in the Churches, S. Clement, &c.

XI. SCULPTURES. On Sarcophagi, in Panels, and STATUES.

XII. THE ANTIQUITIES. According to the Regionary Catalogue of the Fourth Century. Arranged in the XIV. Regiones. And the History of the Churches in the same Topographical Order.

HISTORICAL PHOTOGRAPHS

ILLUSTRATIVE OF

THE ARCHÆOLOGY OF

ROME AND ITALY,

ARRANGED ACCORDING TO THE SUBJECTS.

BY

JOHN HENRY PARKER, C.B.

Hon. M.A. Oxon, F.S.A. Lond. ;

Keeper of the Ashmolean Museum of History and Antiquities in
the University of Oxford, &c.

PART II.

Tombs.
Catacombs.
Castles, Houses, and Towers.
Mosaic Pictures.
Church and Altar Decorations.
Pagan Remains in Churches.
Fresco Paintings.
Sculpture, Pagan, in the Museums.
Christian Sculpture in Churches.
Architectural Details.

LONDON:

EDWARD STANFORD,

CHARING-CROSS.

1873.

PREFACE TO THE TOMBS.

THE number of Roman tombs is so enormous, and their variety of forms so infinite, that it would be absurd to attempt to give any general account of them in a single chapter of moderate length; they would afford ample materials for a volume, or more than one volume. But by limiting my subject to those in Rome itself or in the immediate neighbourhood, the task was not so difficult, and it is useful in more than one respect. The exact localities of the tombs within the wall of Aurelian (which is also the present wall of Rome) is important as indicating the boundaries of the ancient City of the Kings. No tombs have ever been found within the limits of THE CITY properly so called, that is, the line of Servius Tullius, which continued to be the boundary of THE CITY down to the time of Aurelian, A.D. 375, or for nearly a thousand years. It is, therefore, certain that each gate of the City was within the site of the nearest tomb. That of Bibulus is at the east end of the Capitoline Hill, but with a considerable portion of the north-east corner projecting beyond it, so that a portion of the ancient fortress was used to protect the approach to the principal northern gate, and this was the case with the other fortified hills also. It was the custom of the Etruscans, and of other people of the same period as the Etruscan cities, to bury their dead, or at least persons of dis- tinction, on the outer bank of the fortifications, outside of the great wide and deep trench, or foss, that formed a necessary part of the early fortifications. The tomb of Bibulus originally stood on such a bank, and was a detached building, open on all sides, though now hid by houses except on one side. It now stands on the eastern side of the Via di Marforio, which is a modern street in this part; and about a hundred yards to the south of this tomb there is an evident ridge across the street, which is formed by the *agger* or bank and wall of the time of the early kings of Rome. The cellars of the houses in that part of the street which is outside of this ridge have such remains in them as clearly shew that they are built in the great foss, and that the Forum of Trajan extended in that part right up to the foot of the old wall. This tomb, therefore, clearly shews the limit of the City in this direction, and indicates the site of the north-east gate.

B

Other tombs were found by Canina about 1824, in the valley and trench under the Villa Mattei or Celi-Montana, which prove that the southern boundary, with the Porta Capena, was farther to the north than these tombs, and beyond the gorge in the Cœlian Hill, although the mouth of that gorge is close to the spot where they were found. Remains of that southern entrance into the City were also found about a hundred yards to the north of this gorge, during the excavations of 1870.

Two tombs of the first century of the Christian era, or of about the time of Nero, are visible at the east end of the City, one on either side of the great foss or narrow valley that separated the east end of the Cœlian Hill from the Lateran fortress (which was originally a detached fortress, probably made on the Celiolum) : one is on the bank of that fortress, and was probably the tomb of the Lateran family; this is on the eastern side of the trench; the other is on the western side of it, under an arch in the bank, made in modern times to carry the road across the great foss, that bank is now in the garden that belonged to the museum of the Marquis Campana. These two tombs, therefore, fix the eastern boundary of THE CITY, which has been much disputed.

Within the present walls some other tombs of considerable interest remain ; the whole line of the Via Appia, from its commencement at the Porta Capena, in the wall of the CITY, to the outer *mœnia*, where the Porta Appia was made (a distance of just one mile), was lined with tombs on both sides; most of them were too tempting and convenient as building materials, during the Middle Ages, to be left standing; all that remains are the underground parts, considered as foundations only, and these were not worth the expense of digging out as materials. Roman tombs, as is well known, frequently consisted of three chambers, one over the other ; the upper one was above ground, and was used for the family festivals and commemorative feasts, and frequently as a sort of guest-chamber ; in the next chamber, just underground, or half-underground, were the *columbaria*, or pigeon-holes for the cinerary urns, of the bodies that had been burnt ; under this, and considerably underground, was the chamber for the sarcophagi, or stone coffins, for bodies that were buried and not burnt ; in the walls of this crypt there are often *columbaria* also. During the whole of the first century, and sometimes a little before and after that period, the two modes of disposing of the bodies went on simultaneously, some were burnt and others were buried. There are several tombs now remaining visible at Ostia and at Cento-Celle, as well as in

Rome itself, where examples of these two modes of interment can be seen in the same tomb. One of those in Rome is the tomb of Claudius Vitalis, the architect of the Neronian arcade (as I believe), built on the side of the bank on which the arcade passes above; also one of the well-known painted tombs on the Via Latina has both modes of interment. The tomb of the Scipios was for stone coffins only; that ancient family prided themselves on their Etruscan origin, and in keeping up the older Etruscan custom of burying the bodies of the family, and not burning them. One of the tombs of the first century, near the Porta Appia, is usually called a *columbarium*, because the walls are all filled with *columbaria*, or niches. There are many instances of tombs being connected with catacombs. There are several catacombs on the Via Appia and Via Latina under tombs.

The custom of burning the dead bodies only came into fashion in the latter half of the time of the Republic, and did not continue altogether more than three or four centuries; it came in gradually, and went out gradually,—perhaps the Christian repugnance to the practice hastened the abandonment of it.

All people like to give as much publicity as possible to the tombs of their deceased relatives, as may be seen in any churchyard or cemetery; and with the Romans this seems to have been remarkably the case. The Gates of Rome,—not merely those of THE CITY, but those in the outer *mœnia*, on which the wall of Aurelian was afterwards built, — were therefore favourite places for tombs of importance. The tomb of Eurysaces the Baker at the Porta Maggiore is a well-known instance; and in pulling down the Porta Salaria, during the *restoration* of the Walls of Rome in 1870, some interesting tombs were brought to light. One of these closely resembled the tomb of Bibulus, another was the very curious one of the precocious scholar, Quintus Sulpitius Maximus, at the age of thirteen the successful prize-man against fifty-two competitors in Greek and Latin verse, in A.D. 98. The great mausolea of the Emperors Augustus and Hadrian are tombs, although they are also more than tombs. That of Alexander Severus, on the Via Latina, is a regular tumulus, with the chamber of the tomb in it, and a medieval tower built upon it. That of Cæcilia Metella is a landmark to all that part of the country, with the medieval fortification built upon it and round it. From the number of tombs found at Cento-Celle, three miles on the Via Labicana, one of the cemeteries of Rome must have been there in the first century, when that at the Esquiline was abandoned. From the third to the sixth century

B 2

the Catacombs seem to have been the usual cemetery for the middle
and lower classes; the spaces allotted on the sides of the roads
having been previously all sold to the great families.

Some tombs are so closely connected with the Catacombs that·
they might belong indifferently to either chapter in this work.
There is a fine tomb of the first century over the Jews' catacomb in
the Via Appia; the internal arrangement of that tomb is peculiar,
or at least very unusual,—there are niches for images, which are not
likely to have been used in the tomb of a Jew. In one of the
chambers of the catacomb nearly under this is a Pagan sarcophagus,
and painted on the wall of the arch over it is the seven-branched
candlestick, the well-known emblem of a Jew. Putting these things
together, may not some wealthy Jewish heiress in the first century
have married a Pagan, and no distinction of religion being made
after death, both were here buried under this tomb?

The catacomb of S. Calixtus is on the opposite side of the road,
not far from this of the Jews; and there also is a fine tomb of
the second or third century, one side of which has been destroyed,
and the interior of the upper chamber has very much the appearance of one of the Christian chapels usual at the entrance
to the Catacombs; but De Rossi pronounces it a Pagan tomb,
and does not allow that there was any original connection between
this and the catacomb beneath it. Nevertheless, there is a door in
the lower chamber of the right-hand or northern side, which opens
on to the top of a steep flight of steps, descending into one of the
corridors or passages of the great catacomb below in a straight line,
and very steep; the lower part of this has been studiously filled-up,
and another opening made on to the steps sideways, through an
arch or vault cut in the tufa rock, with a very rapid descent into
another corridor in this catacomb, parallel to the first. The present
entrances to these catacombs now in use are both modern, it
seems not improbable that the original entrance was through this
tomb by the side of the road. In the catacomb of S. Agnes
recent excavations, made by the good monks there, have shewn
that no less than five Pagan tombs have openings from them
into it. The upper parts of these tombs have been destroyed, and
the ground above is now occupied by the church and monastery
and the garden of the monks; but the two lower chambers remain
in each case, in the upper of which are *columbaria*, in the lower one
the place for bodies, and in the ground beneath are the catacombs,
which may have belonged to the same families as the tombs: it
seems probable that after each tomb was full, and the family still

went on increasing in numbers, room was wanted for more bodies, and therefore these openings were made into the catacomb or burial-place under each of the tombs.

A class of tombs may be mentioned here, as they are numerous, and are not generally understood. These are built in imitation of the funeral pyre, to which the Romans attached so much importance. The mass of fagots used for burning the bodies is represented by a mass of concrete from ten to twenty feet high, and the great beams of wood which were placed across the fagots in layers, with the ends projecting, are represented by pieces of travertine or of marble, about a foot square, projecting from the concrete mass two or three feet. In most instances these projecting pieces have been chopped off, and carried away for building materials; but portions of them frequently remain, and in some cases they are nearly perfect, as one near Tivoli, and another, not quite so perfect, near the tomb of Cecilia Metella.

Another important use of tombs is for the HISTORY OF ARCHITEC-TURE, the date of a tomb being generally fixed by the inscription found upon it, and many tombs being important structures, quite sufficient to shew the architectural character of the period. To this class belong not only the great mausolea before mentioned, but many of the tombs by the sides of the roads; such as are of brick especially shew the character of the brickwork of the period very distinctly. In our series of photographs there are many fine ex-amples of the brickwork of the best period,—the first century,—especially the time of Nero. The celebrated tomb called *Deo Redi-culo*, in the valley of the Caffarella, is an excellent example of this construction of the best period. Our Chronological List of Tombs supplies also an excellent list of examples of the architecture of each period, from the tombs of the Scipios, B.C. 303, and of Cecilia Metella, B.C. 50, down to the Middle Ages and to modern times.

The Baker's Tomb at the Porta Maggiore is a very curious piece of construction, being built of old stone ovens (?), or an imita-tion of them (?). The tomb of the Imperial family of the Gordiani is a good example of the brickwork of the third century, and that of S. Helena of the fourth, the end of the Imperial period in Rome. After that time we have generally buildings erected of old materials, and rapidly degenerating into the barbarism of the tenth century.

Some of our finest SCULPTURES have come from tombs, whether merely busts of the deceased, or full-length effigies, of which those of the baker, Eurysaces, and his wife, Aristia, are not bad examples of their period; (these should be replaced at the end of the tomb from which they were taken). The numerous half-recumbent effigies belong generally to an earlier period of the semi-Etruscan character. The figure of the precocious youth, Sulpitius Maximus, at the Porta Salaria, is a good piece of sculpture of the end of the first century. A large proportion of the finest panels of sculpture have come from the sides of tombs or of sarcophagi, whether of Pagan mythology or of Christian subjects. For these we must refer to the chapter on Sculpture.

The PAINTED CHAMBERS in the interior of tombs also afford an excellent series of dated examples of fresco-painting. Some of the best that have been preserved in our time are those of the tomb in the garden of the Pamphili Doria; a very remarkable set of the best period, the latter part of the time of Augustus. The painted tombs on the Via Latina of the second century, have also become justly celebrated; there are also some paintings in the sepulchral chamber inside of the pyramid of Caius Cestius, and there are remains of old fresco-paintings in very numerous other instances, but they are not often so well preserved as these. For this subject we must refer to the chapter on Painting.

[The numbers refer to Mr. Parker's Catalogue.]

*Those marked with * are from drawings, valuable for historical purposes,*
but not as photographs.

IN ROME.

Entrance to the Tomb of the Scipios, B.C. 308. *From a Drawing.* 356*
Sarcophagus of Lucius Scipio Barbatus. 336
Tomb of Bibulus, B.C. 84, in the Via Flaminia, at the foot of the Capitol. 1239
Remains of the Tomb of the Gens Claudii, or Family of Claudius, c. A.D. 50, at the foot of the Capitol, opposite that of Bibulus. 1180
Tomb of the Family of the Architect T. Claudius Vitalis, by the side of the Aqueduct of Nero, near the Lateran. 353*
Plans of the two Stories. 355*
Section of the same. Elevation, with two of the Arches of Nero. 354*
Tomb with Columbaria, the wall faced with Opus Reticulatum, in the Exquiliæ, near the Porta Maggiore. 2261
Another Tomb in the Exquiliæ with a series of Columbaria, and some Inscriptions. 2262
The other side of the same Tomb and Columbaria, to shew the original Staircase and Door. 2263
Mausoleum of Augustus. 988
Mausoleum of Hadrian. View. 1085
Plans of the ground and three stories. 188*
Tomb on the Via Ardeatina, between the Bastion of Sangallo and the Thermæ of Caracalla, of the time of Sylla. Interior. 1181

IN ROME, *continued.*

Tomb of the Lateran Family (?) — A Circular Tomb, with two square wings, on the bank of the foss between the Lateran and the Cælian, miscalled the House of Verus. 175
Imitation of a Tomb, with Niches or Columbaria, in the Museum of Campana. 1945
Remains of a Tomb of the first century, near the Porta Latina, within the Gate. 1179
Columbaria of a Burial-club, near the Porta di S. Sebastiano, A.D. 50, in the Vigna Codini. 1462
Another View, with the original Staircase, Busts, and Cinerary Urns remaining in their places. 1178
General View of the Columbaria near the Porta Latina, in the Vigna Codini. 1769
Tomb, with Columbaria of the Servants of Augustus, and other Cæsars, A.D. 20, on the Via Appia, in the Vigna Codini. 1177
Plan of Columbaria for the Servants of the Cæsars. 1298*
Section of the same. 1297*

VIA APPIA.

Tomb of the second century, on the Via Appia. 876
Tomb of the first century of fine brickwork (Opus Lateritium), on the Via Appia Nova, five miles from Rome, near the Villa de' Quintili. 1624

VIA APPIA, *continued.*

Tomb of the First Century, on the Via
    Appia Nova, near the great Piscinæ,
    six miles from Rome.   1037
Tomb on the Via Appia, near Albano,
    a very large mass of concrete, to re-
    present the fagots, and projecting
    pieces of marble broken off, repre-
    senting the timbers of a funeral
    pyre.   1629
Another similar Tomb, with a Medi-
    eval Tower built upon it.   1628
Tomb or Chapel (?) of the third cen-
    tury on the Via Appia, at the original
    entrance to the Catacomb of S. Ca-
    lixtus.   1750
Tomb of the first century, built of fine
    Brickwork, over the Catacomb of the
    Jews.   1755
Tomb of Cæcilia Metella, B.C. 103, with
    the Fortifications and Castle of the
    Gaetani, *c.* A.D. 1310.   361
Doorway of Travertine in the middle
    of the massive concrete wall faced
    with brick.   1360
Tomb of Herodes Atticus (?), called
    Deo Redicolo (*c.* A.D. 140), south
    side.   907
North side of the same.   909
Construction of brick Ornaments, *c.*
    A.D. 140.   908
Construction of Niches, &c.   910

VIA LABICANA.

Tomb of Eurysaces the Baker, and
    his wife Aristia, B.C. 20 (?), close
    to the Porta Maggiore.   598
Effigies of Eurysaces and his wife
    Aristia.   882
Tomb, with Columbaria of the time
    of Sylla, in the Thermæ of the Gor-
    diani, B.C. 60.   932
Details of the same.   933
The same, with the Well.   934

VIA LABICANA, *continued.*

Exterior of the Tomb of the Gordiani
    in their Thermæ, A.D. 240.   925
Interior of the same.   898

VIA LATINA.

Fine Tomb of the first century, of re-
    markably good brickwork, on the
    Via Latina.   1430
Another fine brick Tomb on the Via
    Latina.   705*
Plan and Section of the same.   706*
General outlines of the patterns on the
    Vault and on the Walls.   708*
[For the beautiful decorations of this
    Tomb, see Fresco Paintings and
    Stucco Ornaments, of which there
    are a complete Series of Photo-
    graphs from 2091—2103.]
Mausoleum or Tomb of S. Helena,
    A.D. 330. View of the Exterior.   207
View of the Interior.   208
Plan of the Mausoleum.   206*
Pyramid of Caius Cestius, near the
    Porta S. Paolo, *c.* A.D. 10.   652

VIA FLAMINIA.

Tomb of the Naso Family, five miles
    on the Via Flaminia, called Tor di
    Quinto.   1635
Tomb on the Via Claudia, with an In-
    scription to P. VIBIVS MARIANVS of
    the time of Severus, miscalled the
    Tomb of Nero.   1634
Remains of the Porta Salaria in March,
    1871, and of a Tomb, closely re-
    sembling that of Bibulus (?).   2069
Cippus of Quintus Sulpitius Maximus
    (found buried in the southern tower of
    the Porta Salaria).   2070
Remains of a Circular Tomb of the first
    century in the northern tower.   2071

PHOTOGRAPHS OF THE
TOMBS IN CHRONOLOGICAL ORDER.

Tomb of the Scipios, B.C. 303.   356*
—— of Cæcilia Metella, B.C. 60.
    361, 1360
—— and Columbaria, of the time of Sylla, B.C. 60, on the Via Prænestina.
    932, 933, 934
—— on the Via Ardeatina.   1181
—— on the Via Appia.   1628, 1629
—— of Bibulus, B.C. 34.   1239
—— of Eurysaces the Baker, B.C. 20.
    598, 882, 1463*
—— or Pyramid of Caius Cestius, A.D. 10.   652
—— in the garden of the Villa Pamphili-Doria, on the Janiculum, of the time of Augustus, with Columbaria, and a curious and remarkable series of fresco drawings in good preservation.   2695 to 2708
—— at the Porta Salaria, B.C. 30 (?), or A.D. 22 (?).   2069, 2071
—— of Sulpicius Maximus, at the Porta Salaria, A.D. 90, with the Greek and Latin verses.   2070
—— with Columbaria of the Servants of the Cæsars.   1177
—— Section of the same.   1297*
—— Plan of the same. ·   1298*
Columbaria of a Burial Club, A.D. 50.
    1462, 1178, 1766, 1767, 1768, 1769, 1770, 1771, 2261, 2262, 2263
Tomb of the Lateran Family (?).   175
—— in the form of a Temple, in the porch of S. Lorenzo.   320
—— of the Cavia Family (first century).   1748
—— of the first century.   1037, 1179, 1430, 1431, 1624, 1639, 1755
—— of the Gens Claudii or family of Claudius, A.D. 50.   1180

Tomb of the family of the Architect, T. Claudius Vitalis, c. A.D. 50. Plans and Sections.   353*, 354*, 355*
—— of the Naso family.   1635
—— on the Via Latina, A.D. 60.
    705*, 706*, 708*
—— of the Aterii, A.D. 50.   1500, 1501
—— of Titus Flavius Verus.   85
—— of Agrippina.   91
—— in the Villa Campana, A.D. 100.
    1942
—— of the second century on the Via Appia.   876
—— of Hadrian, A.D. 130.   1085
—— of Hadrian, Plan.   188*
—— called Dio Ridicolo, c. A.D. 60, miscalled of Herodes Atticus, A.D. 140.   907, 908, 909, 910
—— of Statilius Aper, c. A.D. 150.
    1021
—— painted, on the Via Latina, second century.   2091, 2095, 2098 to 2104
—— on the Via Appia, second century.
    876
—— of the Gordiani, A.D. 240. 923, 925
—— on the Via Claudia, miscalled the Tomb of Nero.   1634
—— Heroum of a deified Emperor, in the Thermæ of the Gordiani.   898
—— of S. Helena, A.D. 330.   207, 208
—— Plan.   206*
—— of the third century on the Via Appia.   1750
—— Columbaria in the Villa Campana (an imitation).   1945

TOMBS IN CHURCHES.

Tomb of Cardinal Alfanus, A.D. 1150.
    312

Tomb of Cardinal Fieschi, A.D. 200,
A.D. 1256.   597
—— of Cardinal William de Bray, A.D.
1280.   1701
—— of third century, afterwards of
Monsignor Spinelli.   315
—— of Friar Museio da Ramora, A.D.
1300.   1645
—— of Pandulphus Savelli, A.D. 1306.
2268
—— of Cardinal Adams of Hertford,
A.D. 1398.   1702
—— of Cardinal D'Alençon, A.D. 1408.
1911
—— of Cardinal Terrici, A.D. 1428. 651
—— of Nicolas da Forca Palena,
A.D. 1449.   1398
—— of Brother Bartholomeus Caraffa,
A.D. 1450.   316
—— of Cardinal Astorgius, A.D. 1451.
650
—— of Cardinal Fortiguerra, A.D. 1473.
1703
—— of Cardinal d'Ansio, A.D. 1483.
1646
—— of Antonius Pullarius and his
Brother, A.D. 1498.   1929

Tomb of the Archbishop of Ragusa,
A.D. 1505.   1392
—— of Cardinal Ascanius Sforza,
A.D. 1505.   2280
—— of Cardinal J. B. Savelli,
A.D. 1520.   2267
—— of Cardinal A. J. Venerius,
A.D. 1579.   2073
—— of a Bishop, in the Church of
S. Prassede, A.D. 1350.   1484
Tombstones in the Cloister of S. Croce
in Gerusalemme.   401, 402, 403

Loculi in Catacombs.   1183, 1222,
1223, 1283, 1611, 1621
Tombstones from Catacombs.   1257,
1259, 1384, 1594, 1595, 1596, 1906,
1907, 1908, 1909, 1910.

Tomb at Pompeii, B.C. 100 (?).   2161
—— of the Ghirlande, Pompeii.   2156
—— Views of, at Pompeii.   2160
—— on the Via Romana, Ostia.
1826, 1827

So many popular delusions are current on the subject of the Roman Catacombs, that it is difficult to obtain a hearing for a plain, unvarnished tale, in which the truth has been the only object sought for. These popular delusions are not confined to one party or one side, there are extremes both ways, and both are equally erroneous; they have unfortunately been made use of as weapons of polemical controversy, and the conclusions wished for on each side have been jumped at without proper examination of the foundations on which they are built. The same tests must be applied to the legends respecting them that are applicable to all other legendary history, and they cannot be received as authentic without examination.

The origin of the name of Catacomb, to begin with, is one of the questions long discussed and still undecided; but as the name is medieval only, and not that by which they were originally called, it does not seem very material: the original name was *Cemeteria*, and like many other words this had a double signification, one general, the other specific; the general name was that of a tract of ground applied for the purpose of interment, the specific name was a particular burial-vault, called also a *cubiculum*, which was usually sold in perpetuity to a particular family, without reference to the religion of its members. In one instance only, as far as has been ascertained, it was given to the holders of a particular office; the bishops of Rome in the third century had their own special cemetery or burial-vault, in the general burial-ground of the family of Calixtus. S. Anicetus, bishop and martyr, A.D. 174, and Bishop Soter, A.D. 189, were buried in this Catacomb; and Bishop Zephirinus in his own cemetery, *near that* of Calixtus; on the Via Appia. S. Calixtus himself was not buried in the cemetery that bears his name, but in that of Calepodius on the Via Aurelia.

The Chronological Table of the Catacombs given in this Chapter, brings out their history more clearly, and shews how frequently they have been restored; and a comparison of the fresco paintings in them with the mosaic pictures in the churches, which are all dated, shews that the paintings are not of so early a date as is commonly supposed; they generally belong to the latest restorations, the gilt glass vases found in them give the same evidence; few of them are of any early date, and many of them are not Christian. This is another indication that many of the catacombs were family burial-places, and that there were no exclusions or consideration of religion after death. There were three catacombs for the Jews, and one for the Gnostics, or the worshippers of Mithra; and the last was connected with those of the family of Prætextatus.

There is a very general misunderstanding on the subject of sand-pits; those who are accustomed to English sand-pits only cannot easily understand how very different the Roman sand-pits are, from the peculiar geological formation of the Campagna of Rome, the whole of the subsoil of which consists of successive layers of tufa of different degrees of hardness; one hard layer is good for building-stone, another is only loose sand called Pozzolana, a third is between the two. The last kind of tufa is the best for the purpose of cata-combs, but they are by no means all made in that material: some are in clay, others in river sand, which is quite different from the Pozzolana. The sand-pit roads were made by excavating, in a bed or layer of sand, a space sufficient to allow a horse and cart to go along, and the sand dug out to make the road was itself a sand-pit, but there are other pits at intervals also. These subterranean roads formed very convenient modes of access to the Catacombs, which were generally made in the harder bed of tufa under that level. In some cases the beds are alternate, the Pozzolana is found at two or three different levels. In the catacomb of S. Priscilla, which is five stories deep, two are sand-pit roads, one of which has been partially used for burials, the other has not. When these roads passed under the property of a family, whether their farm or their burial-place, the ground was the property of that family to any depth, and the name of *prædium* would apply equally to both.

HISTORICAL PHOTOGRAPHS ILLUSTRATIVE OF
THE CATACOMBS.

[*The numbers refer to Mr. Parker's Catalogue.*]

---

*Those marked with * are from drawings, valuable for historical purposes,*
but not as photographs.

I. CHRONOLOGY (pp. 14 to 24).

Early Tombstone with Greek Cross under a round Arch, and Inscription from S. Cyriaca, *c.* A.D. 300.   442

S. Agnes—Inscriptions on Tombstones, built into the wall of the staircase of the Church.   1594, 1595

S. Calixtus—Inscriptions of Pope Damasus, 1. over the Altar in the Chapel of the Popes; 2. in the Chapel of S. Eusebius.   1795, 1811

II. THE MARTYRS (pp. 25 to 35).

In S. Calixtus — Inscriptions on the Tombs of the Bishops or Popes.
Anteros, A.D. 236.   1797
Fabianus, A.D. 249.   1798
S. Cornelius, A.D. 253.   1799
Eutychianus, A.D. 283.   1796

In S. Agnes. Maximus.   1596
In S. Prætextatus. Januarius.   1821

III. CHAPELS OF THE MARTYRS (pp. 36 to 46).

S. Sebastian—Section and Plan of the Crypt or Platonia.   483*, 484*
Ancient Chapels at the Entrance to the Catacomb, *c.* A.D. 350 (?), and 772.   285, 286, 287, 288

IV. CONSTRUCTION (pp. 38 to 46).

A Natural Section of part of the Catacomb of S. Cyriaca, in the burial-ground of S. Lorenzo f. m., in three parts, shewing an arco-solium, or place for a Sarcophagus, with paintings in the arch, and the junction at an angle of two corridors, with the loculi, or graves in the walls.   1131, 1132, 1133

S. Agnes—Cubiculum, with Columns, and place for the Altar.   626

S. Prætextatus—A Brick Cornice and Wall of the first century, with another wall of the fourth, of stone and brick, built up against it, and a Brick Arch of the second.   1618, 1619, 1620

S. Domitilla—Brickwork of the first century, at the Entrance.   620

S. Pontianus—Corridor and Staircase at the entrance, restored A.D. 858—867, by Pope Nicholas.   611

S. Cyriaca—Corridor with Loculi.   1282

S. Prætextatus—Doorway and Loculi of early character.   1621

S. Generosa—Well at the Entrance.   1224

V. VIA CORNELIA, AURELIA, AND PORTUENSIS (pp. 56 to 67).

FRESCO PAINTINGS[1].

S. PONTIANUS.

Head of Christ, A.D. 858—867. 607 A

The same, from Perret's Drawings.
463*, 607 B*

Baptism of Christ, A.D. 858—867.
608 A

—— *from Perret's Drawing.* 608 B*

Painting of a Jewelled Cross, A.D. 858—867. 609 A

—— *from Perret's Drawing.* 609 B*

Painting of SS. Marcellinus, Pollion, and Petrus, A.D. 858—867. 610 A

—— *from Perret's Drawing.* 610 B*

Christ crowning S. Abdon and S. Sennen, with figures of S. Milex and S. Bicelus, A.D. 858—867, *from Perret's Drawing.* 471*

Jewelled Cross and two Saints, S. Miles and S. Pymenius, A.D. 858 —867, *from Perret's Drawing.* 474*

S. GENEROSA,
At the College of the Arvales.

A Loculus or Tomb cut in the rock and left unopened. The aperture is covered by three tiles fixed with plaster, and in the plaster are graffiti or inscriptions scratched in the plaster when wet, of the fourth or fifth century. 1222

Another Tomb unopened, with the tiles and graffiti on the plaster. 1223

Loculi, with the bones remaining in them, c. A.D. 500. 1183

Head of Christ from the painting in fresco, c. A.D. 600. 1159

VI. VIA OSTIENSIS, ARDEATINA, APPIA, LATINA (pp. 68 to 91).

S. DOMITILLA—Brickwork, c. A.D. 100, with a Well and a Vase(?) or Font(?), called a Baptistery, at the entrance. This Catacomb is part of the great one called SS. Nereus and Achilleus. 621

Well near the entrance. 1819

Cubiculum, with Fresco Paintings of the Four Seasons, c. A.D. 250(?), Spring and Autumn. 618, 619, 1820

The Adoration of the Magi, A.D. 523, *from Perret's Drawing.*
1613 from nature, 465*

The Madonna, A.D. 523, *from Perret's Drawing.* 466*

SS. NEREUS AND ACHILLEUS.

A Christian Sarcophagus, at the entrance to the Catacomb. 1815

Pagan Inscription of Tiberius Claudius Claudianus, found there. 1817

Christian Inscription, written on the reverse of that of Tiberius Claudius Claudianus, ÆMILIO, etc. 1818

Tombstone, with Inscription, c. A.D. 320, CERONTI VIBAS IN DEO. 1617

Loculus, unopened. The aperture is covered by a tile, on which is rudely painted an inscription, IANVARIVS COIVCI FECIT, with a palm-branch at each end. 1611

Painted Chamber, A.D. 523. The ceiling is flat and painted in panels, with birds and flowers; under the arch of the cubiculum is a vase with two birds and two palm-branches. The flat soffit of the arch is also painted in panels. 1615

---

[1] The Fresco Paintings in the Catacombs *are taken with the magnesian light,* which has an appearance similar to moonlight. The Cardinal-Vicar, who acts in the name of the Pope, has now (in 1870) forbidden any more to be taken, on the pretext that the smoke from the magnesian lamp might injure the frescoes. All that was important had been taken before this order was issued. A few of the same subjects have also been taken from Perret's drawings, to shew how much the modern artists have developed and improved upon the originals.

SS. NEREUS, &c., *continued.*

The Good Shepherd. The figure is represented in shepherd's dress, with a lamb on his shoulders, and two sheep at his feet, with flowers in the usual manner. 1616

The Adoration of the Magi. The Madonna is seated, with her right hand uplifted ; on her left Christ is represented not as an infant, but as a boy, as at Ravenna, and other Byzantine examples. There are four Magi, two on either side, in order to complete the picture and fill the space under the arch of a cubiculum. The Magi wear the Phrygian cap, and have offerings in their hands. 1613

A Feast or Agape. This may represent the Last Supper, as is usual, but it appears more like a family feast ; some of the heads appear to be those of mere boys. It is under the arch of a cubiculum. 1614

The head of a youth, in a circular frame, probably a portrait of the defunct. 1609

An Orante, with a sheep. 1816

A group of figures, to whom one is preaching. 1612

S. PRÆTEXTATUS.

Plan and Section of a Corridor. 744

Brickwork and Doorway at the Original Entrance, *c.* A.D. 100. 616

Fragment of a Sarcophagus with Bas-relief, and Painted Vault of Chapel, *c.* A.D. 200. 614

The Cultivation of the Vine. 1822

THE GNOSTICS (?), or Worshippers of the Persian God MITHRAS.

Fresco Paintings, I. a Warrior -kneeling, and a woman crowned with laurel, and of a Man raising a dead Lamb and pointing to some Stars in the Heaven ; 2. Seven priests of Mithras seated at a table (SEPTE PII SACERDOTES). In the centre is the priest VINCENTIVS. He and two others wear the Phrygian cap. This

THE GNOSTICS, *continued.* ·

Catacomb was in communication with that of Prætextatus on the Via Appia. 1791, 1794

Arch, with an Inscription over a Cubiculum (not now legible). 1623

A Warrior holding a lance, between a Genius and a Man. 1792

Four figures engaged in some ceremonial (very indistinct), fourth century (?) or later(?). 1281

Fresco. The good angel introducing a woman, called VIBIA, to several persons. Over them is written INDUCTIO VIBIES. Under the Arch are six figures, with Vibia in the centre, and over their heads the inscription BONORUM IVDICIO IVDICATI. 1793

S. CALIXTUS.

The Cover of the largest marble Sarcophagus discovered in the Catacombs, said to be that of Pope Zephyrinus, A.D. 218. 1810

Sarcophagus, the sculpture representing Genii, the Resurrection of Lazarus, and Daniel in the Lions' Den. 1807

Fresco Paintings of the Seasons, in a Cubiculum. 1808, 1809

Chapel of the Sacraments. A *fossor*, or grave-digger, Abraham and Isaac in attitudes of prayer, a ram, and a bundle of firewood. 1806

A figure seated holding a scroll, and another figure drawing water from a well, said to be Christ and the woman of Samaria. 1801

History of Jonah, I. coming out of the mouth of the sea-serpent (or whale); 2. thrown by the sailors into the sea. 1802, 1803

Seven figures upon a tricliniar bed. There are two dishes with fish, and eight baskets loaded with bread. 1804

A *fossor*, or grave-digger. In another part of the picture a small table, or tripod, upon which is a dish with fish and bread. A man, Christ,

S. Calixtus, *continued.*

after the Resurrection (?), extends the right hand over the fish, and on the other side is a female figure in the attitude of prayer. The Church (?).
1805

An Orante said to be S. Cæcilia (ninth century), of our Saviour and of S. Urban, Pope, with the Inscription SCS VRBANVS. 1800

Figures of S. Cornelius, Pope and Martyr, S. Xystus II., Pope (SCS XYSTVS PP ROM), and of S. Optatus, Bishop. 1813, 1814

VII. Via Labicana, Nomentana, Tiburtina.

SS. Peter and Marcellinus.

The Adoration of the Magi, A.D. 772—775, *from Perret's Drawing.* 627 C*

Adoration of the Magi. Two of the Magi only are shewn, there not being room for more. 2116

An Agape or Commemorative Love Feast, with the names over the heads of the figures. 2117

An Agape with this inscription, AGAPE . MISER NOBIS. There are two children at the table. 2118

Christ seated between two Apostles (?), standing and addressing Him. He has the nimbus, they have not; their dress resembles the surplice and stole. At the foot is the Holy Lamb standing on Calvary, with other Apostles (?). 2119

A female Orante, with two members of her family, A.D. 772(?). 2115

S. Agnes.

Paintings of an Orante, with the Good Shepherd, A.D. 772—775. 628

The Blessed Virgin and Child, A.D. 772—775. 627 A*

—— *from Perret's Drawing.* 627 B*

S. Cyriaca.

A female Saint, richly attired and crowned, A.D. 772—795, *from Perret's Drawing.* 468*

S. Cyriaca, *continued.*

Madonna, and S. Catharine, *c.* A.D. 772—795, *from Perret's Drawing* 479*

Figure of S. Cæcilia, A.D. 772—795, *from Perret's Drawing.* 472*

Three Loculi, closed with Tiles: 1. With Stamp and small Vase; 2. With Skeleton and Palm-branches; 3. With Inscription, the Labarum of Constantine, an Anchor, a Dove with Palm-branch, *from Perret's Drawing.* 481*

A Painted Vault, *from Perret's Drawing.* 482*

Tombstone of Antonia Cyriace, with a dove and olive-branch on each side of the name, *c.* A.D. 250, taken from this Catacomb and built into the wall of the Church of S. Giorgio in Velabro. 1257

Three Skulls, and a brick stamp found with them, with inscription— OF(*ficina*) S(*exti*) DOMI(*tii*) SATVRNINI [A.D. 264?]. 1283

S. Hermes.

Fragment of Mosaic Picture representing Daniel in the Lions' Den, A.D. 577, the only Mosaic Picture now remaining in the Catacombs. 629

VIII. Via Salaria Vecchia, and Nova (pp. 108 to 118).

SS. Saturninus and Thrason— Paintings in the lowest story, of the time of Pope Hadrian I., A.D. 772—795. 1751

Three Loculi, with Paintings of Jonah, Moses striking the Rock, bird with foliage, and two female Orantes, *from Perret's Drawing.* 467*

An Orante, a lady richly attired, with lace borders and a veil, A.D. 772—795. 1774

—— *from Perret's Drawing.* 475*

Another Orante, A.D. 772—795. 1775

—— *from Perret's Drawing.* 476*

SS. SATURNINUS, &c., *continued.*

Head of the defunct, with a Bird and Flowers, A.D. 772. 1752

Jonah under the ivy-bush (according to the Vulgate version, the gourd in the English version), A.D. 772—795. 1777

Moses striking the rock, A.D. 772—795. 1776

The Good Shepherd, and a Figure holding a Scroll or Book, with the inscription, DORMITIO . . . . . . [Silvestri (?)]. 1778

—— *from. Perret's Drawing.* 480*

Tobias presenting a Fish to his Father. 1779

An Orante, with an Ordination (?) on the right, and a Madonna on the left, *from Perret's Drawing.* 469*

S. PRISCILLA.

The Madonna addressed by a Prophet, who is expounding the Scriptures to her, with the Star of Bethlehem (?) above, A.D. 523. 1467

—— *from Perret's Drawing.* 470*

Painted Chapel, restored by John I., A.D. 523. 612

Stucco Ornament in a Chapel. 613

The three youths in the "burning fiery furnace," and Orantes, *c.* A.D. 523. 1468, 1471

Painting of an Orante or female figure erect, in the Oriental attitude of prayer. On her left hand a Madonna (?) or mother and child, on her right hand three figures, one seated, the others standing. The interpretation given to this group is an ordination. *Other interpretations are given to this picture.* Also a graffito of the name of BOSIVS. 1470

An Orante addressed by two persons standing and pointing on her left hand, with another figure standing, wrapt up in a tunic, on her

S. PRISCILLA, *continued.*

right. (Allegorical interpretations are given to this group.) 1472

Seven men carrying a wine-cask, *c.* A.D. 523, with graffiti of the names of ANTONIVS BOSIVS, ORATIVS DE NOBILIBVS, &c., and a tombstone with the inscription — BONAVIÆ COIVGI SANCTISSIMÆ. 1469

Graffiti. 1473

Two Loculi, unopened, with letters painted on the Tiles, which cover the openings. 1474

A Peacock, with tail expanded and Diaper Ornaments, A.D. 523, *from Perret's Drawing.* 477*

A Peacock, side view, A.D. 523, *from Perret's Drawing.* 478*

IX. CATACOMB OF THE JEWS ON THE VIA APPIA. (p. 119).

Part of the Place for Washing the Bodies at the entrance, with Arcosolia or Arched Tombs partly rebuilt in the fourth century. 1753

Staircase at the exit. 1754

A Painted Cubiculum, *c.* A.D. 150, *taken with the magnesian light.* 773

Painting of Birds, A.D. 150, in the same chamber. 562

The same, from a Drawing by Ewing. 1161*

View in a painted Burial-vault, *taken with the magnesian light.* 774

The same, from a Drawing by Ewing. 1160*

Pegasus, a Painting on the Wall, *c.* A.D. 150. 775

A Peacock, A.D. 150. 561

Fragment of a Pagan Sarcophagus, A.D. 150. 563

Inscriptions, with Emblems. 776

C

XI. CATACOMBS OF NAPLES (pp. 126—129).

Views of the Ospizio de' Poveri di S. Gennaro.   2143, 2144

Construction under the Portico of the Ospizio de' Poveri di S. Gennaro, at the entrance to the Catacombs, with very bold corbelling.   2145

General View of the entrance to the Catacombs, with Frescoes on the walls.   2146

General View of the entrance to the Catacombs.   2147

Fresco Paintings in the Catacombs, representing SS. Desiderius and Agutius, eighth century (?).   2148

Fresco Paintings in the Catacombs, representing two Saints, and a lily between them.   2149

Fresco Painting in the Catacombs, representing a peacock, vases, and flowers.   2150

Fresco Painting in a niche on the right-hand side of the entrance to the Catacombs.   2151

Column, with Inscription, in the Catacombs.   2152

Chair of S. Gennaro, cut in the Tufa rock of the Catacombs.   2153

Those within the Catacombs are taken with the magnesian light.

XII. CHURCHES OUTSIDE THE WALLS.

S. PAUL'S (pp. 130 to 134).

View of the Interior before the fire. 456*

——— after the fire, in 1823, shewing the parts that were left standing. *These two are from scarce Engravings.*   623*

View of the Cloister, thirteenth century; exterior, with Cosmati work and Inscription.   2020

——— Interior, with light shining through the Arcade.   2019

Paschal Candlestick ornamented with rich Sculpture.   2018

Altar Canopy or Baldachino, details of.

Frescoes in the Cloister.   2024 to 2030

Inscriptions.   1985 to 2030

Mosaic Pictures.   2031 to 2037

S. SEBASTIAN'S (pp. 138 to 141).

Exterior of Apse, *c.* A.D. 850 (?).   289

Plan of Church and Monastery, with the Chapels at the entrance to the Catacomb.   819*, 341*

Views of the Ancient Chapels at the Entrance to the Catacombs, *c.* A.D. 850(?), and 772; and a Porticus.   285, 288

S. URBAN'S (pp. 142 to 144).

Altar of Bacchus found there.   1365

The Classical Portico, *c.* A.D. 50, filled up with modern brickwork.   1590

Exterior View behind the Altar, with fine brick cornice.   1364

S. HELENA OR S. PETER AND MARCELLINUS (p. 145).

Plan.   206*

View of the Exterior and Interior.   207, 208

S. AGNES (pp. 146 to 148).

View of the Exterior, with the Porch of the twelfth century, the Apse, A.D. 623, and the Campanile.   1589

Interior, with the Canopy over the Altar or Baldachino, the Classical Columns and the Apse, with the Mosaic Pictures, A.D. 626.   1591

The Gallery or Triforium, and the Clerestory, with the Ceiling and the Fresco over the Arch.   1592

Mosaic Picture.   1593

Fresco Painting.   1597

Inscriptions.   1594, 5, and 6

S. CONSTANTIA (p. 149).

Interior, *c.* A.D. **320**. This view shews the coupled or twin columns standing upon a plinth ; the central part of the floor has evidently been raised to the same level. It was probably built for a Baptistery, with tombs or sarcophagi, and altars in the aisle round, the vault of which is enriched with Mosaic pictures. 1600
The Mosaic Pictures. 1607, 1608

S. ALEXANDER (pp. 151 to 153).

View in the Church. 384
Antique Columns. 385
Perforated Marble Screen. 383

S. LORENZO (pp. 154 to 159).

General View of the Exterior, with Portico and Campanile. 1082
Interior of the Nave, from the west, with antique Arch of Triumph, and Mosaics. 592
Wall of side aisle, Exterior, *c.* A.D. 750 ; and Wall of Clerestory with early Plate-tracery, A.D. 1216. 322

Interior, Antique Columns in the North Aisle of the Choir. 594
Altar and Canopy, A.D. 1160. 593
Campanile, *c.* A.D. 1216. 319
Cloister of the Monastery, *c.* A.D. 1216. 321
Cloister, *c.* A.D. 1320. 1093
Ambo and Paschal Candlestick and Ionic Capitals to antique Marble Columns. 595
Early Pagan Sarcophagus, *c.* A.D. 200, representing a Nuptial ceremony, with Canopy, *c.* A.D. 1256, made into the Tomb of the Cardinal Fieschi. 597
Sculpture of Lions at the door. 317
Sarcophagus, with shallow Sculpture of the Vine, &c. 318
Tomb in the form of a Temple. 320
Fresco Paintings of the legend of S. Stephen and S. Lorenzo, or Laurence (?), in the porch. 1120 to 1126

S. STEPHEN (p. 160).

Remains of the Church. 2105

It will be observed by those who know the topography of Rome, that nearly all the Gardens and Palaces, and Thermæ, are in the space between the old wall of the City, the boundary of Servius Tullius (which continued to be the boundary of THE CITY, strictly so called, for a thousand years), and the outer *mœnia* on which the great wall of Aurelian was afterwards built: this outer line was *then* made the boundary of the City, but this was not until near the end of the third century of the Empire and of the Christian Era.

This great district is about a mile in width on the average, and thirteen miles long on the outer edge, and it was always to a great extent occupied by these gardens and palaces, and places of public amusement. It had been much intercepted by the fosses or trenches of the early fortifications, many portions of which were conveniently made into the Circuses, other portions were filled up and built upon, and others made into reservoirs for the aqueducts. This district was called the *Pomœria* in the fifth century, as we know from Sidonius Apollinaris (in the passage quoted in my chapter on the Walls and Gates). It had been previously called the *Pomœrium*, at least, this must have been one meaning of that word, and although that name was given also to the municipal boundary, that is not at all inconsistent with the other use of the name. The *cippi* of Augustus, who restored those of Sylla, have been found in the outer line of this district, or the *mœnia* of the old City, upon which the Wall of Aurelian was afterwards built, and on the outer bank of the great foss of the *mœnia*, after the addition to the City made by Sylla, who had enlarged the *pomœrium*. It is most probable that he added to the outer line by extending the *mœnia* so far as to include the Pincian Hill on the north, on which his own palace or castle was built, and that large tongue of land to the south beyond the line of the Marrana, which runs in the bed of the river Almo. This stream had served as a wet ditch to the City on the south side to the corner of the Aventine, the cliffs of which then became the defence, and were so high that they did not require any outer *mœnia*. For this reason there was no *pomœrium* to the Aventine, until the time of Claudius, of whose wall and double gate we have remains. The private house or palace of Trajan, and the Thermæ of Sura his cousin, were made on the

Aventine, and we have remains of them. They were probably the seat of the family to which Trajan belonged, and they covered a large part of the Aventine proper, not the Pseudo-Aventine, or southern part of the Aventine. That portion had been the Arx or Citadel of the Aventine when that hill was a separate fortress, and the eastern division of it was occupied by the house of Cilo and his gardens, of which also we have remains identified by an inscription found upon them.

The great tongue of land or promontory added by Sylla, was occupied by the Thermæ of Severus and Commodus, just within the Porta Latina, and those of the Antonines, called after Antoninus Caracalla. On the southern side of the Cœlian were the house and gardens of Seneca, of which there are remains. This garden now belongs to the hospital of the Lateran, to which it was given at a very early period. The cliff of the Cœlian was the boundary of the City in this part. Eastward of the Cœlian were the house and gardens of the Lateran family and of the Asinii, and the Sessorium with its gardens, the residence of the imperial family of Varius, and afterwards of S. Helena. Northward of this, on the eastern side of Rome, were the great Thermæ of the third century, made in the gardens of Mæcenas, which had previously been the Exquiliæ. Recent excavations on this ground have shewn the tombs with *columbaria*, and traces of the aqueducts, and remains of these great thermæ, to which the building called the Minerva Medica was one of the halls of entrance. Beyond this was the Prætorian Camp, and further to the north were the gardens of Sallust, afterwards of the emperors from Nero to Aurelian, now the gardens of Mr. Spithoever, and the Villa Ludovisi. The building in these gardens, called the "Temple of the Vestal Virgins," was probably a *nymphæum*, or hall of the Thermæ of the Emperors. There are some remains of the house of Sallust under that of Mr. Spithoever, especially an aqueduct of the first century and a reservoir for it.

PHOTOGRAPHS ILLUSTRATIVE OF THE
EARLY AND MEDIEVAL CASTLES, HOUSES, AND TOWERS.

[The numbers refer to Mr. Parker's Catalogue.]

Those marked with * are from drawings, valuable for historical purposes, but not as photographs.

THE FOSS-WAYS.

The Via Appia, just within the Porta Appia, with the Arch of Drusus standing in the foss-way, taken from the banks on the western side, shewing the foss-way from above, with the banks on each side of it, supported by walls. 1203

Section of the Porta di S. Lorenzo, shewing the different levels and the filling up of the foss-way. 1291*

Plan and Sections of parts of the Wall of Rome, shewing the difference of levels within and without, and the foss-way on the exterior. 1292*

Temple of Romulus, the son of Maxentius, now the church of SS. Cosmas and Damian, built in the Via Sacra when that was a foss-way, shewing the upper part of a marble column, the lower half of which is buried by filling up the road ; the doorway has been moved from the lower church, now the crypt, which is at the original level. 268

Temple of Pallas, shewing the upper half of the columns of the time of the Emperor Nerva, A.D. 96 ; the lower half buried by filling up the foss-way of the Forum Transitorium. 271

HOUSES.

House of Sallust, part rebuilt, A.D. 85. 1018

—— Entrance to the Temple(?) or Nymphæum(?) of the Gens Flavia, A.D. 85. 1020

—— Remains of the Porticus Milliariensis of Aurelian. 1022

House of Fabius Cilo on the eastern cliff of the Aventine Hill (now S. Balbina—this was ascertained by an inscription found upon it). 1190

House of Seneca against the cliff, western side of the Cœlian.—View. 132

—— Plan. 1158*

Villa and Garden of the Domitii (now the Villa of Mr. Esmeade). 2062

Private House of the Emperor Hadrian (miscalled the Villa of Asinius Pollio). 630, 631, 725, 726

—— Plan of the same. 1110*

Private House of the Emperor Trajan and Thermæ of Sura. Remains of wall on the Aventine (789), of pits (1747), painting in a subterranean chamber. 2107, 2108

THE LATERAN.

Plan of the ancient House, now incorporated in the Wall of Rome, the Pontifical Palace, Church, Baptistery, and Hospital. 38*

—— Sections, Longitudinal and Transverse. 699*

—— View of Medieval Wall across the old foss on the northern side. 39

—— Original Postern - gate incorporated in the Wall of Aurelian. 40

—— Wall on part of the North Front, now the north-east angle. 41

—— Tower, with part of East Front. 42

This view also shews stones from the Wall of the Kings, piled against the foot of the tower by Belisarius to protect it against the battering-rams of the Goths (see Procopius). They were removed in 1871, during the *restoration*(?) of the Wall.

LATERAN—Hall of the Palace of Plautius Lateranus, with brick arches of peculiar construction (now a yard for fowls).   174

—— View of the Eastern Angle.   41

—— Tower and Windows of the first century, now in the Wall of Rome. 971

—— Tomb of the Lateran Family (?), on the bank of the foss between the Lateran fortified Palace and the Cœlian Hill. (This is popularly miscalled the House of Verus.)   175

—— View of the Modern Church and Palace, now the Museum, shewing also the great bank and foss of the old earthwork.   1320

—— View of the Exterior, incorporated in the Wall of Rome from the Marrana, shewing also the situation of the Gate.   1309

—— View from the Cœlian across the foss, with a Medieval Column placed upon an ancient Cippus at the southeast corner of the old City.   1322

—— Gateway of the Lateran Hospital, A.D. 1446.   892

JANICULUM FORTRESS.
—— foss, looking up.   956
—— foss, looking down.   957
(See also Diagrams of the Walls and Gates of Rome, Plate VII.)

VATICAN FORTRESS, ancient scarped cliff on south side, with wall of Sangallo built up against it. 958, 959

—— Ancient scarped cliff on north side, with Medieval tombstone inscriptions cut upon it.   3090, 3091

Lavacrum of Agrippina on the Viminal, remains in 1871.   181, 182

HOUSE OF PUDENS. Plan of underground chambers.   177*

—— Plan on the surface of the ground.   176*

—— Outer Wall of the Basilica or Great Hall, c. A.D. 20, now the church.   178

—— Underground chambers. 1733, 1734

HOURDS. Remains of a Hourd on the east Wall of the Pretorian Camp.   14

—— In the Wall of Rome, near the Porta di S. Lorenzo.   25

—— On the Tower of the Anguillara Family.   230

MEDIEVAL HOUSES AND CASTLES.

TOWER OF THE CAPOCCI, now of S. Lucia in Selci.   245

—— of the Cesarini, now of S. Francesco di Paola.   246

—— of the Conti. Plan and Section.   888*

———— Plan of Site.   238*

———— View.   237

Torre Delle Milizie.   239

—— Millina.   1333

—— di Pier Leoni.   164

HOUSE OF THE CRESCENTII,—called also Monzone,—Palace of Pilate,—House of Cola di Rienzi.   248

—— of the Bonadies Family, with Loggia.   249, 250

HOUSE OF THE ANGUILLARA FAMILY.
———— Plan.   231*, 887*
———— View.   230

HOUSE OF THE ALBERTESCHI.
———— Towers.   233
———— Details.   234, 235, 236
———— Plan.   232*

HOUSE OF THE MARGANA FAMILY.
———— Plan.   242*
———— View of Gate and Tower. 243
———— Front to Court restored. 244*

House of the Fornarina. Window and balcony.   801

CASTLE OF THE GAETANI or Caetani Family, with Tomb of Cæcilia Metella. Plan.   258*

—— View, with the Tomb.   259, 361
—— Church or Chapel.   260
—— Details of the Church.   425
—— Walls of the Medieval Castle.   360, 362

CASTLE OF THE FRANGIPANI.
Remains of the Priest's house of the twelfth century, adjoining to the small church of S. Sebastiano in Pallaro, originally the chapel of this Castle. 308

CASTLE OF THE SAVELLI
(now S. Sabina).
—— Plan. 240*
—— View from the Clivus Publicius. 241
PALACE OF S. MARK OF VENICE,
A.D. 1464. Plan of upper and lower
Palace. 257*
—— Views of the east front. 252, 599
—— West Front and Façade of S.
Mark's Church. 253
—— The Northern Court (unfinished,
shewing also the side of the church
with two towers). 255

VENETIAN PALACE.
—— The Southern Court (A.D. 1468—
1494). (This is highly finished, and
very elegant.) 256
—— View from the upper part, now
the monastery of Ara Cœli. 581, 582
—— Details. Doorway, A.D. 1480. 600
—— Window, A.D. 1480. 601

House of the Cardinal, now the Re-
formatory of S. Balbina. 278
House of Cardinal Bessarion, A.D. 1450,
near the church of S. Cesareo, with
a Loggia or Porticus. 1192

PREFACE TO MOSAIC PICTURES, &c.

THE object of this chapter is to shew the application of the Fine Arts to the decoration of churches by the early Christians, and during the Middle Ages in Rome. It was at first intended to have divided it into two chapters, but they were found to be so closely connected together that it was better to include both in one. With the help of friends who have paid more attention to this branch of the subject than I have done, I believe that it is now fairly worked out as far as the limits of one chapter will allow, although (as in other parts of this work) there is material enough for many volumes. This chapter in fact contains the substance of the great work by Ciampini on Mosaics, still the best work on the subject; while several other books are referred to, as will be seen. A sketch of the mosaics of the time of the Early Empire and before the Christian era is given as a necessary introduction. It is indeed impossible to separate them during the first three centuries and the early part of the fourth, as there are both mosaics and frescoes of that period respecting which it is impossible to say whether they are Pagan or Christian.

The mosaic pavements of the early period are often really pictures just as much as if they were intended to be placed against the walls. That mosaic pictures were also placed upon walls, we have the evidence of Pliny, together with remains of them on walls and vaults. There are many mosaic decorations on walls at Pompeii, though no actual pictures; these are always in fresco or in distemper colour. The incised marble slabs, with pieces of marble of different colours inserted, though not strictly mosaic, are closely allied with it. Of these we have a fine example in a chapel of the church of S. Antonio Abbate, originally taken from the house of Junius Bassus of the time of Constantine, but here used for the decoration of a Christian chapel. This branch of the art has been revived of late years, and has been used by Salviati in the Royal Chapel (originally Wolsey's chapel) at Windsor with good effect, although unfortunately the style of the drawing adopted by him is not consistent with the architecture of the building. Other mosaics are introduced in the vault and the upper parts with marvellously fine effect. Mosaics were occasionally used for tombstones, of which we have a few examples only remaining; they were also largely used for inscriptions, and with excellent effect. Texts of Scripture executed in mosaics might very well be revived in our English churches; as there is an idea of permanence presented to the mind by mosaics that is particularly suitable for the decoration of churches. In London, especially, a picture that can be washed is much better suited for use in a church than any other. On the roofs and vaults or ceilings, where washing would be difficult and inconvenient, frescoes or distemper paintings might be used and renewed from time to time, as was done with the Catacomb pictures.

The mosaic pictures on the walls and the vaults of the apses in the churches of Rome extend from the fourth century to our own time. Those made for the family of Constantine in the mausoleum and baptistery of Constantia are the earliest that can be called Christian art, and they are still among the best. They are evidently the work of Pagan hands, well skilled in the art, and were therefore long supposed to shew that this Christian baptistery had been a temple of Bacchus, as the cultivation of the vine and the manufacture of wine happen to be there represented; but the frequent mention in Scripture of the vine and its branches would of itself justify the retaining of this subject by the early Christians. We find the same subject also in the Catacombs, where it *may* have been Christian also and used in time of persecution. It will be observed that the subjects of the mosaic pictures are always Scriptural until the sixth century; no figures of saints or martyrs, not Scriptural, are found before that period, nor any representation of the Madonna as an object of worship. In all the early paintings of the Madonna the subject is the strictly Scriptural one of the adoration of the Magi; in the shop windows of modern Rome the figure of the Madonna seated, originally the centre of the group, is however frequently seen alone, with the figures of the Magi omitted. Perhaps the earliest Madonna known, as a separate figure, is the one in the corridor, now a sentinel's path, in the wall of Aurelian near the Porta Appia (now di S. Sebastiano), supposed to have been made by the Greek soldiers under Belisarius, at the time of the siege of Rome by the Goths; the painting, with the foliage ornament in the margin, agrees with that period.

A comparison of the mosaic pictures in the churches with the paintings in the Catacombs, shews clearly, by the style of drawing, that three-fourths of these paintings are of the eighth or ninth century; of the remaining part a considerable proportion is of the sixth, of the time of John I., who became bishop and pope, A.D. 523.

This pope made one cemetery or catacomb and *restored* two others, and we have the same subjects and the same style of painting in all three. Other paintings, earlier than the fourth century, are not of religious subjects at all, and cannot therefore be called Christian : hey are merely ornamental and nothing more. Of mosaics of the ;ixth century we have so few remaining in Rome, that we must go to Ravenna to see the style of drawing of that period.

The church of S. Prassede, in the ninth century, has preserved more of such decorations than any other church in Rome, and the effect is very fine, especially that of the two triumphal arches over the altar, the one in front, and the other at the back of the transept, or central space, with the apse or tribune behind it, all covered with mosaic pictures. Yet, notwithstanding the great effect of this decoration, when examined in detail, it is seen to belong in reality to a bad period of art. The finest mosaic picture in Rome is said to be that over the altar in the church of S. Pudentiana, but this has been so much tampered with in the seventeenth century, when the church was rebuilt from the foundations, and when probably the present apse, on the wall of which the mosaic picture is placed, was built, that we can have no confidence in it for the history of art, unless it is of the art and skill of the mosaicists of the time of the Renaissance. Ugonius, who saw the church rebuilt, picked up the monogram of Pascal from among the fragments on the ground, which proves that at least part of it was of the ninth century. The first example that we know of placing figures under arches in a mosaic picture, as if in a series of niches, is in S. Francesca Romana, also of the ninth century. At that period a school of Greek artists was established in Rome.

Of the tenth century, we have no example remaining of a mosaic picture, and the only frescoes of that period are the side pictures in the church of S. Urbano, in the Caffarella, (the pictures at the two ends have been restored, those on the sides have not), which are very much of the character of some of the Catacomb pictures.

At the end of the eleventh and the beginning of the twelfth century a great revival took place in art. Of this period we have the remarkable frescoes of Beno de Rapiza, in the church of S. Clement, now in the crypt or subterranean church, though they were not so at the time they were painted : they were then on the level of the eye of a person standing on the floor of the church, but the level of the floor was raised when the upper part of the church was rebuilt in the beginning of the twelfth century, after the raid of Robert Guiscard and his Normans. who had burnt the roof, and damaged the walls so much, that it was necessary to rebuild all the upper part of it: the opportunity was taken to raise the floor to the same level to which the road outside had been raised, by the filling-up of the old foss-way, at the low level of which the church had been originally built.

In the thirteenth century, we have the remarkable mosaic picture at S. Maria in Trastevere of the Madonna seated on the same throne with Christ. The art of that period is good, and better still towards the end of that century or the beginning of the fourteenth. Of this period we have also the fine mosaic pictures in the apses of the Lateran and of S. Maria Maggiore, and the very remarkable picture in the portico or *loggia* over the principal entrance of the latter church, representing the dream of the pope and the senator, and the miraculous fall of snow in July in Rome. Of this period we have also the fine mosaic pavements called *Opus Alexandrinum*, the work of the Cosmati family, and the beautiful ribbon mosaic ornaments in nearly all the church furniture of that period. Some of the tombs executed by these admirable artists are perhaps the finest Christian tombs that we have anywhere. This beautiful art is not confined to internal decoration, for we have an example of it signed with the name of Deodatus Cosmati on the Cœlian Hill, on the gateway of the monastery of the Redemptorists, representing Christ between a black and a white slave. This work has not suffered from the long exposure to all weathers, although it is in an exposed situation. The interiors of the two deserted churches of S. Cesareo and SS. Nereo and Achilleo, on the Via Appia, have also preserved some of the finest examples of Cosmati work. Another very fine example has been carefully restored in S. Lorenzo beyond the walls.

The Pagan remains used in the Christian churches, enumerated by Mons. de Montault, are extremely curious and interesting, and very little known. The signatures of medieval artists is also a new subject for English people. The excellent account of the Cosmati family will be also new to most persons, as those who are generally well acquainted with such subjects have only heard of the Cosmati work, and know but little about them.

The mosaic pictures at Ravenna seem almost a necessary complement to the subject, as they supply an admirable series for a period of which we have very little in Rome.

HISTORICAL PHOTOGRAPHS

ILLUSTRATING TESSELLATED PAVEMENTS AND MOSAIC PICTURES IN ROME.

FROM MR. PARKER'S COLLECTION.

[The numbers refer to Mr. Parker's Catalogue.]

ANTIQUE OR CLASSICAL PERIOD.

BEFORE THE CHRISTIAN ERA, AND FIRST CENTURY.

FIRST PERIOD.

The Celebrated PLINY'S DOVES, from the Original in the Capitoline Museum. 1695

This was discovered by Cardinal Furietti, in the Villa of Hadrian, at Tivoli. It is believed to be that made by Sosus, for the pavement of a house at Pergamus, and described by Pliny (lib. xxxvi. c. 25, al. 60).

Curious Mosaic found at Porto d'Anzio, now in the Capitoline Museum. 1696

The subject is Hercules, spinning for love of Omphale, who is represented by a Cupid, while a lion is being tied up by other Cupids. This mosaic expresses the proverb "Omnia vincit amor."

SECOND PERIOD.

Pavement with Reticulated or Net-like Pattern. 378

Excavated in 1869 in the Vigna Guidi, in the private house of Hadrian (?).

Another Pavement in the same place and of the same kind, with figures, vases, birds, &c. 545

Another of the same, with Birds and Tritons. 1700

Other Pavements from the same, representing Marine Monsters, Tritons, &c. 630, 725

Excavated in 1867.

Mosaic Pavement and Fountain, from the Guard-house of the seventh cohort of the Vigili, in Trastevere, excavated in 1867. Representing Marine Monsters, &c. 640

Mosaic Pavement in a House of the time of the Antonines, excavated in 1873, near the Via dei Serpenti, on the line of the Via Nationale (now destroyed). 2970

It is of black and white marble, in diamond-shaped patterns.

Mosaic Pavement, with the heads of the four Seasons, from Ostia, now in the Church of S. Paul at the Tre Fontane. 3065

Mosaic Wall Picture, representing a group of figures and some allegorical subjects, found at Cento-Celle by Guidi in 1866. 1857

Another, from the same place, of a comic mask adorned with a diadem and a crown of flowers. 1858

(There was a great cemetery in the time of Hadrian at the place now called Cento-Celle from the hundreds of cells and tombs found there.)

Mosaic Pavements in the Lavacrum of Agrippina, A.D. 20. 2121, 2122

Mosaic Picture representing the Delivering of Hermione from the Monster, now in the Villa Albani (696) 2806

It was found at Atina, near Arpino.

Mosaic Inscription at the entrance of
the Tomb of Pomponius Hylas,
c. A.D. 50.   1221
Mosaic Picture found in the Villa of
Hadrian, representing the combat of
a lion and a bull (Cent. II.), now in
the Vatican Museum (125).   2508
Another from the same, representing
goats in a meadow (Cent. II.), now
in the Vatican Museum (113).   2505
Mosaic Picture representing a shield
dedicated to Minerva, in the middle
of which is the head of that Goddess,
now in the Vatican Museum (558).
                                      2608
Mosaic Picture representing the god
Silenus, with the usual attributes,
found at Ostia, now in the Lateran
Museum.   2895
Mosaic Pavement, representing Gladiators, now in the Lateran Museum.
                                      2852
Found in 1825 in the Thermæ of

Caracalla, where other fragments of it
were uncovered in 1871.

THIRD CENTURY AND BEGINNING
OF THE FOURTH.

View of a Harbour with the miraculous draught of fishes(?), on a
Tombstone from the Catacombs. 1384
Mosaic Pavement of the third century
in black and white, discovered in the
year 1869 near the Trinità de' Pelle-
grini, representing Mercury with a
Nymph in the centre, and heads of
the four Seasons.   254
Opus Sectile—A Tiger on the back of
a Calf, now in the church of S. Antonio Abbate.   1460
(This is considered by De Rossi to
have been part of a great mosaic picture, made to illustrate the triumphal
entry of Constantine into Rome. It
was formerly thought to be much
older.)

MOSAIC WALL-PICTURES IN THE CHURCHES.

FOURTH CENTURY.

S. CONSTANTIA, on the vaults of the aisle
round it, *c.* A.D. 320. This remarkable and celebrated series of Mosaics
is the earliest *series* that is known, and
the present excellent set of photographs is the first that has been taken
of them. Among the subjects represented are the heads of Constantine
and his family; the cultivation of the
vine, and the vintage. Oxen are represented drawing cart-loads of grapes,
and among the branches of the vine
are little figures of genii, birds, flowers,
vases, &c. This is believed to be an
allusion to the text of Scripture, "I
am the Vine, ye are the branches."

Some good Roman antiquaries con-
sider that this church was built by
the children of Constantine after his
death, and that A.D. 350 is more
likely to be the correct date than
A.D. 320. It was at one time considered as a temple of Bacchus; but

the sarcophagus of Constantia, which
was found here, and removed to the
Vatican Museum, shews that it was
her burial-place, and, as she was a
Christian, she would not have been
buried in a pagan temple. It is believed to have been also a Baptistery.
1601, 1602, 1603, 1604, 1605, 1606

FIFTH CENTURY.

S. MARIA MAGGIORE—Side Pictures in
the nave, over the arches and under
the clerestory windows, representing
a series of forty Scripture subjects,
chiefly the history of the patriarchs.
The whole series is taken from Ciampini's great work.

"The name of Pope Sixtus III. is
in the mosaic at the top of the arch,
and seems to apply to the whole
series of pictures, not only to those
on the arch, but to those on the side
walls also, of which twenty-seven of

S. MARIA MAGGIORE.

the original pictures are said to remain; some have been restored in the sixteenth century. The figures retain the antique Roman type and costume, the heads are much the same as those on the Column of Antoninus, and the toga preserves its cut and its ancient folds; but the heads are too large for the bodies. They are thick, short, and clumsy; the lines are undecided, the composition confused. Nevertheless, real art still appears here and there : thus, in the second picture, Abraham separating from Lot, the arrangement of the scene is not unskilful; the figures express well what they are about, and one feels that the two groups are separating. The fourth picture, Isaac blessing Jacob, has almost the same *pose* as Raphael has given to it in one of the compartments of the Loggia. The taking of Jericho and the battle with the Amalekites also have details which are not without a certain interest. Everything is not lost, therefore, in works of that period; there remain some gleams of spirit and truth, some traces of the old traditions mixed up with negligence, clumsiness, and ignorance almost incredible." (M. Vitet.)

—— The Arch of Triumph, A.D. 432—440. *From Ciampini, Plate* 49. 1951*
N.B.—*Under the arch, Ciampini has inserted the jewelled throne and small busts of the Madonna.*
N.B. *The series of side pictures begins from the choir on the left hand.*
—— Side Pictures, A.D. 432—440. *From Ciampini, Plate* 50. 1952*
1. Melchizedec offering bread and wine to Abraham (Gen. xiv. 18).
2. Abraham and Lot part asunder (Gen. xiii. 9).
—— *From Ciampini, Plate* 51. 1953*

S. MARIA MAGGIORE.

1. Abraham entertains three angels (Gen. xviii. 2); Sarah at the door of the tent (Gen. xviii. 10). A.B.C. the Angels, D. Abraham, E. Sarah, F. the bread prepared, G. the bread on the table.
2. Isaac blesses Jacob; and Esau returns from hunting (Gen. xxvii. 29, 30). A. Isaac, B. Esau, C. Rebecca, D. Jacob.
The same, from the original ª. 2038
—— *From Ciampini, Plate* 52. 1954*
1. Jacob and Laban (Gen. xxix. 10). A. Laban, B. Rachel, C. Jacob, D. Leah.
The same, from the original. 2039
2. Laban, Jacob, and Rachel (Gen. xxix. 25). A. Laban, B. Rachel, C. Jacob.
The same, from the original. 2040
—— *From Ciampini, Plate* 53. 1955*
1. Jacob returns to Laban and demands Rachel; the nuptials of Jacob and Rachel (Gen. xxix. 28, 29). A. Laban, B. Rachel, C. Jacob, D. Bilhah.
The same, from the original. 2041
2. The separation of Laban and Jacob (Gen. xxxi. 2).
The same, from the original. 2042
—— *From Ciampini, Plate* 54. 1956*
1. Separation of the flocks of Laban and Jacob continued; Jacob takes his wives Rachel and Leah (Gen. xxxi. 17).
The same, from the original. 2043
2. Jacob's message to Esau (Gen. xxxii. 3); the meeting of Jacob and Esau (Gen. xxxiii. 1). A. Esau, B. Jacob, C. Attendants.
The same, from the original. 2044
—— *From Ciampini, Plate* 55. 1957*
1. Hamor and Shechem, Dinah, Jacob, and his sons (Gen. xxxiv. 25). A. Hamor, B. Shechem, C. Jacob,

ª These photographs from the original mosaic pictures of the fifth century were taken at night with the magnesian lamp; it was not practicable to take them in any other manner. All that were sufficiently perfect were thus obtained.

S. MARIA MAGGIORE.

D. E, and F. The sons of Jacob, D. Hamor, E. Shechem, G. Simeon, H. Levi.

The same, from the original.   2045

2. Jacob reproaches his sons (Gen. xxxiv. 30). A. Jacob, B. Simeon, C. Levi.

Jacob is sent to Bethel (Gen. xxxv. 1, 2).

The same, from the original.   2046

—— *From Ciampini, Plate* 56.   1958*

1. The marriage of Moses with Zipporah (Exod. ii. 21) ; Moses keeps Jethro's flock of sheep (Exod. iii. 1).

2. Moses found by Pharaoh's daughter, who sends for a nurse (Exod. ii. 5). A. Pharaoh's daughter, B. The mother of Moses, C. and D. Attendant damsels.

3. Moses accused before Pharaoh (Exod. ii. 14, 15). A. Moses, B. Jews accusing him, C. Pharaoh on his throne, with attendants.

—— *From Ciampini, Plate* 57.   1959*

1. The return of Moses to Egypt (Exod. iv. 20).

2. The meeting of Moses and Aaron (Exod. iv. 27). A. Moses, B. Aaron.

—— *From Ciampini, Plate* 58.   1960*

1. Moses and the Golden Calf (Exod. xxxii. 20).

2. Moses delivers the Ten Commandments (Exod. xxv. 1, &c.).

The same, from the original.   2047

3. Quails and manna sent to the Israelites (Exod. xvi. 13, 14).

—— *From Ciampini, Plate* 59.   1961*

1. The passage of the Red Sea (Exod. xiv. 21—26).

The same, from the original.   2048

2. The battle of Israel against Amalek, who is overcome by the lifting up of the hands of Moses (Exod. xvii. 8—12).

The same, from the original.   2049

—— *From Ciampini, Plate* 60.   1962*

S. MARIA MAGGIORE.

1. Moses striking the rock produces water (Exod. xvii. 6).

The same, from the original.   2050

2. Moses gives the books of the Law to the Levites (Deut. xxxi. 9).

The same, from the original.   2051

3. The ark carried before Joshua (Joshua iv. 18).

—— *From Ciampini, Plate* 61.   1963*

1. The rebellion of Korah, Dathan, and Abiram (Numb. xvi. 1, 19—41).

The same, from the original.   2052

2. Joshua leads the people of Israel (Joshua i. 16) ; Rahab receives and conceals the two spies, and lets them out of the window (Joshua ii. 15).

The same, from the original.   2053

—— *From Ciampini, Plate* 62.   1694*

1. The men carry the twelve stones before the ark in the Jordan (Joshua iv. 8); the spies go into Jericho (Joshua ii. 1).

The same, from the original.   2054

2. The siege of Jericho (Joshua vi. 1, 2).

The same, from the original.   2055

—— *From Ciampini, Plate* 63.   1965*

1. The walls of Jericho fall down. The ark carried round the city with trumpets (Joshua vi. 20).

The same, from the original.   2056

2. The sun and moon stand still before Gibeon (Joshua x. 13).

The same, from the original.   2057

—— *From Ciampini, Plate* 64.   1966*

1. Joshua fights against the Amorites. The Lord smites them with hailstones (Joshua x. 10, 11).

The same, from the original.   2058

2. The five kings brought out (Joshua x. 23).

SIXTH CENTURY.

SS. COSMAS AND DAMIAN, on the Tribune, A.D. 526—530.   1441

Christ stands on the clouds, with the roll of the Gospels in His left

SS. COSMAS AND DAMIAN.

hand, His right hand elevated as in the act of speaking.

—— Two figures to the right of Christ. S. Peter introduces S. Damian, with his crown of martyrdom in his hand. Behind S. Damian is S. Felix, with the model of the church in his hand, as being the founder; but this figure is a modern restoration.   1442

—— Two figures on the left of Christ. S. Paul introduces S. Cosmas, with his crown of martyrdom.   1443

—— S. Theodorus stands under a palm-tree behind S. Cosmas; he also has his crown.   1444

—— Three of the sheep under the figures.   1445

The central one has the nimbus, and stands upon the rock, with the four rivers of Paradise flowing from it; the other two are looking at Him with great attention. Over the head of the central sheep, or Christ, is the name of the river IORDANES.

SEVENTH CENTURY.

S. AGNES, on the Tribune, A.D. 626.   1593

There are three full-length figures. In the centre is S. Agnes, attired in a Greek costume, richly ornamented with beads; she has a nimbus, and holds in her hand a roll or book. On her right is Pope Symmachus, with a model of the church as the builder of it: and on her left Pope Honorius, with a book in his hand in a richly-jewelled cover. Both of the Popes are attired as bishops, in surplice, cope, and stole; the stoles have tassels and crosses worked upon them. Over their heads is the hand of God in the heavens, surrounded by clouds and stars. On the soffit of the arch is a cross in the circle, with stars and scrolls of ribbon.

S. PIETRO IN VINCOLI — Figure of S. Sebastian, A.D. 682 (?).   1931

(Ciampini, *Vetera Monimenta*, pars

ii. p. 114, and tab. xxxiii.; Paulus Diaconus, *De Gestis Lombardorum*, lib. vi. c. 5.)

ORATORY OF S. VENANTIUS in the Baptistery of S. John in Fonte, near the Lateran, A.D. 639—642.   1709

Emblems of the Four Evangelists, the Holy Cities, figures of S. Anastasius, Asterius, Tellius, Paulinianus on one side; Maurus Septimius, Antiochianus, Gaianus, on the other. Most of these saints belong to the fifth century.

Head of Christ, with Angels adoring, and figures of S. Paul, S. Peter, S. John the Evangelist, S. Venantius, and Pope John IV., holding the model of the Chapel, and Theodorus I., holding a book; in the centre, the Madonna in the attitude of prayer.   1710

Mosaics in the Chapel of S. Venantius in the Baptistery of S. John in fonte (A.D. 639—642).   1338

Mosaics in the Chapel of S. Venantius in the Baptistery of S. John in fonte (A.D. 639—642).   1339

S. STEFANO ROTONDO. A jewelled cross, with the head of Christ in a medallion above, and figures of S. Primus and S. Felicitas.   1925

EIGHTH CENTURY.

THE MADONNA from Old S. Peter's, now in the Sacristy of S. Maria in Cosmedin, A.D. 705.   638

S. PUDENTIANA.

—— Picture on the Vault of the Apse or Tribune of, with details.   1417

Represents the Court of Heaven; Christ seated on a Throne, richly attired; the Apostles, in surplice and stole (?), seated each in front of his Gate, with the Martyrs, Pudentiana and Prassede, standing behind them; Buildings of Ancient Rome, a jewelled cross, and emblems of the Evangelists in the background.   280

The left-hand side represents five of the Apostles, and S. Prassede with the crown of martyrdom in her hand. In the background, buildings of the heavenly Jerusalem, and in the clouds the emblems of two of the Evangelists—the angel and the winged lion, with the jewelled cross in the centre.   1416

Right-hand side, five Apostles and S. Pudentiana (?), with the crown of martyrdom in her hand; above are the emblems of two Evangelists—the winged bull and the eagle.

(The remaining two Apostles are concealed by the modern cornice, or destroyed.)

S. Pudentiana, jewelled cross and emblems of the Evangelists in the clouds, over the picture of Christ and the Apostles.   1418

——— The central figure of Christ on His throne, the right hand giving the benediction; in the left, the book with the words   1419

DOMINVS CONSERVATOR ECCLESIÆ PVDENTIANÆ.

Over His head the jewelled cross, and on either side the emblems of the Evangelists.

There is great difference of opinion as to the date of this Mosaic Picture in the apse of S. Pudentiana, one of the finest in Rome. The historical evidence is in favour of the eighth century; but connoisseurs say the work is too good for that period, when the church was in ruins, and was rebuilt, as we are told in Anastasius. It was again rebuilt in the sixteenth century by the Gaetani family; at that time the monogram of Pope Hadrian was found by Ugonius among the fragments then lying on the ground, and also the capital letters in mosaic, forming the name from another inscription. The monogram may have been from the Arch of Triumph over the altar, which is not always of the same age

as the apse; but this would not apply to the capital letters. The name of Siricius (who was Pope from 384 to 397) occurs on an inscription built into the side wall of the choir, but this is not part of the apse.

The picture was probably made up of fragments of different periods in the sixteenth century. There is evidently a great deal of patchwork in it, and the figure of Christ, with the inscription, is not of the same age as the figures of the Apostles.

The Triclinium of Charlemagne at the Lateran, *c.* A.D. 800, as restored.   761

NINTH CENTURY.

S. MARIA IN DOMNICA, on the Apse, A.D. 818.   1926

The Madonna, with a crowd of Saints on either side, and a small kneeling figure of Pope Paschal I., the donor, and his monogram in the crown of the arch.

(Anastasius, Biblioth., 435 : Ciampini, *Vetera Monimenta*, pars ii. p. 142, 143, and tab. xli.)

——— Mosaics in the Apse — General View.   1927

S. PRASSEDE OR PRAXEDES, A.D. 820.

Interior of the Nave, shewing the Altar, with its Canopy or Baldacchino, the Apse, and the two Arches with Mosaic Pictures.   1477

——— Summit of the inner Arch, with Christ and figures of Saints and Martyrs, and the Monogram of Pope Paschal I.   1478

——— Right-hand side of outer Arch, Figures of Saints and Martyrs. 1479

——— Figures on the left-hand side of the Apse.   1480

Pope Paschal with the square nimbus, and the model of the Church in his hand. S. Prassede, with her crown of martyrdom in her hand, led by S. Paul towards Christ, whose figure appears on the right of the picture. Six of the sheep under the figures.

——— Central group of Apse.   1481

Christ stands in the river Jordan, with the name ✠ IORDANES under His feet. He has the cruciform nimbus, and the roll of the Gospels in His left hand. His right is raised in the attitude of benediction. Over his head is the hand of the Almighty Father. On his right, S. Paul introduces S. Prassede ; on his left, S. Peter introduces S. Pudentiana.

S. Prassede. Figures to the left of Christ in the Apse. 1482
S. Peter introduces S. Pudentiana, followed by S. Zeno, each carrying the crown of martyrdom. Under the feet of the figures are five more of the sheep and the city of Bethlehem.

—— Outer Arch, right-hand side. 1483
"The Noble Army of Martyrs," each in a white robe, with his crown of martyrdom in his hand.

—— Monogram of Pope Paschal. 1506
In the centre of the soffit of the inner arch. On the surface, the Lamb on an altar, and angels worshipping.

—— Outer Arch, left-hand side. 1507
"The Noble Army of Martyrs," each in a white robe, with his crown in his hand extended before him. Above are emblems of the Evangelists.

—— Chapel of S. Zeno—Front. 1508
A series of heads in circles. Christ and the Twelve Apostles in the outer circle, the family of Pudens in the inner one, and, at the foot, on each side, the heads of the donors—the Colonnas. The architecture is made up from antique fragments.

—— Chapel of S. Zeno—Window. 1509
On either side SS. Peter and Paul, and, over the window, the throne of God richly jewelled.

—— Chapel of S. Zeno—Vault. 1510
One of the four angels supporting the bust of Christ in the centre of the vault.

—— Chapel of S. Zeno—Side. 1511
Window with Mosaic ornament,

and the figures of SS. Prassede and Pudentiana, each carrying a crown of martyrdom.
Window with Mosaic ornament, and figures of SS. Pudens and Hermes, with their crowns. 1512

S. CECILIA IN TRASTEVERE—Apse of the time of Paschal I., A.D. 820, with his Monogram on the Arch. 1706
In the centre is Christ, erect, in the attitude of blessing in the Oriental manner, holding in the other hand a scroll. On the right, S. Paul, S. Cecilia, and S. Paschal ; on the left, S. Peter, S. Valerian, and S. Agatha. Over the head of Christ is a hand holding a wreath, and under His feet a lamb with six sheep on either side, emblematical of the Saviour and the Apostles.

S. CONSTANTIA over a door. 1607
This picture represents Christ seated on the globe, attired in a flowing robe. In His left hand He holds a roll or book. His right is elevated, and holds out some object to a Saint, who, kneeling to Him, offers a palm-branch. On His left are seven palm-trees.

—— Over another door. 1608
In this picture, Christ is represented standing in the clouds, with His right hand elevated, as calling attention. In His left is a scroll, with the words DOMINVS PACEM DAT. This scroll He presents to the prophet, who receives it eagerly. On His left hand is another prophet, admiring. Under His feet are the four rivers of Paradise, and two sheep on each side. At each end of the picture is a tumulus, with a palm-tree.

TWELFTH CENTURY.

S. MARIA IN TRASTEVERE—General View of the large Central Picture in the Tribune, *c.* A.D. 1150. 1915
Christ and the Blessed Virgin seated on one throne, the hand of

the Almighty Father in the clouds above, and figures of Apostles and Saints on either side.

At the time this mosaic was made, S. Bernard said enthusiastically that the physical beauty of Christ surpassed that of angels, and that it was an object of admiration and an occasion of enjoyment to those celestial beings [b].

Picture over the Porch, the wise and foolish virgins, A.D. 1139.   459*

S. Maria in Cosmedin—Mosaic Pavement, "Opus Alexandrinum," A.D. 1120.   635

THIRTEENTH CENTURY.

Mosaic Picture representing Christ between two Slaves, one black, the other white, over the Door of the Church of the Redemptorists, on the Cœlian, the work of Deodatus Cosmati, with his name inscribed.

340, 1948

MAGISTER JACOBVS CVM FILIO SVO COSMATO FECIT HOC OPVS.

BAPTISTERY OF S. JOHN IN FONTE, Chapel of SS. Cyprian and Justina.
1725

S. CHRISOGONUS IN TRASTEVERE — The Madonna, with SS. Chrysogonus and Jacobus, c. A.D. 1210.   1860

S. CLEMENT — Apse, or Tribune, and Arch of Triumph.   1274

Inscriptions under the great picture in the apse, c. A.D. 1250—1274:

✠ ECCLESIAM CHRISTI VITI SIMILABIMVS ISTI.

DE LIGNO CRVCIS JACOBI DENS IGNATII QVE IN SVPRASCRIPTI REQUIESCVNT CORPORE CHRISTI.

✠ QVAM LEX ARENTEM SED CRVX FACIT ESSE VIRENTEM.

Inscription on the Arch of Triumph, c. A.D. 1120; left hand, by the side of the figure of S. Paul,

AGIOS PAVLVS.

Under the figure of S. Laurence:—
DE CRVCE LAVRENTII PAVLO FAMVLARE DOCENTL

By the side of the figure of Isaiah his name, ISAIAS. On a scroll, or open book in his hand, this text, c. vi. :

VIDI DOMINUM SEDENTEM SUPER SOLIUM.

On the right hand, S. Peter

AGIOS PETRVS,

and S. Clement, both seated ; under them is this inscription—

RESPICE PROMISSVM CLEMENS A ME TIBI CHRISTVM.

Below, Jeremiah holding a scroll, on which is written the text, HIC EST DOMINUS NOSTER, ET SUSTINEBIMUS ILLUM.

At the foot, on each side, are the holy cities, and under the principal picture are the sheep, as usual at the period.

S. MARIA MAGGIORE, in the external Loggia, A.D. 1299.   1414

Christ seated on His throne ; with His right hand giving the benediction, and in His left a book, with the words,

EGO SVM LVX MVNDI.

He has the cruciform nimbus, jewelled, and the monogram XC ; on his throne is a rich cushion. The picture is represented as in a circular panel carried by four angels ; under it are the arms of the Cardinals James and Peter Colonna, and this inscription of the artist, Filippo Russuti—

PHILIPPVS RVSVTI...FECIT HOC OPVS.

—— in the external Loggia at the east end, A.D. 1299.   1423

The Left-hand side of the picture represents Pope Liberius (A.D. 352), and John, the Roman Patrician, each

---

[b] S. Bernard, Serm. II., domin. prim. post octav. Epiph., among his works, Bened. edit., t. i. col. 807. Id. Serm. I., in fest. omn. Sanct., ibid., col.

1023. See also Eméric-David, *Histoire de la peinture au moyen âge*, p. 33. Paris, 1842, post 8vo.

having the same dream or vision of the Madonna, and of the snow-storm in the month of August ; with very characteristic furniture of rooms, decoration of windows, and other ornaments, and a contemporary inscription under the picture, giving the date of it, A.D. 1299.

—— Right-hand part. 1424
Representing different parts of the legend, the snow-storm in August, with the snow left on the ground, marking out the site of the Church, with John the Patrician, the Pope, Bishops and Clergy assembled ; and in another part, the Patrician John going to narrate to Pope Liberius the vision he had seen.

OLD CHURCH OF S. PAUL, outside the Walls. Fragments and Details of Mosaic Pictures.
—— The conventional Head of S. Paul, A.D. 1243—1250. 2031
—— The conventional Head of S. Peter, distinguished by the hair on the beard of peculiar cut, A.D. 1243—1250[c].
2032
—— Another Head of S. Paul, A.D. 1243—1250 (?). 2033
—— Mosaic Picture of a Swan. 2034
———— a Bird on a Tree. 2035
—— Mosaic Picture of a Bird. 2036
—— Mosaic Picture of a Bird. 2037

S. MARIA IN TRASTEVERE. The Apse, on the wall under the Tribune, by Cavallini, A.D. 1290. 1912
A Madonna in a medallion, with S. Paul holding a drawn sword, and S. Peter with his hand on the head of a small kneeling figure, Bertoldo de' Stefaneschi, by Cavallini.
Inscription under the medallion :—

VIRGO DEVM COPLEXA SINV
SERVANDA PVDOREM
VIRGINEVM MATRIS FVNDANS
PER SECVLA NOMEN

RESPICE COMPVNCTOS ANIMOS
MISERATA TVORVM
—— on two panels on the right-hand side. 1913
1. The Offerings of the Magi ;
2. The Presentation in the Temple.
—— on two panels on the left-hand side. 1914
1. The Blessed Virgin seated on a throne, receiving the Annunciation ;
2. The Assumption of the Blessed Virgin.

FOURTEENTH CENTURY.

S. JOHN IN THE LATERAN. Pavement of the Church, called *Opus Alexandrinum*, work of the Cosmati family, c. A.D. 1306, with the arms of the Colonnas as the donors (a column crowned). 1711
Head of Christ, with angels worshipping, from the apse or tribune. 1749
Mosaic Tomb in the pavement of the Nave of the Church of S. Sabina. 1645
Representing Friar Museio da Ramora, eighth general of the order Dei Predicatori, who died in the year 1300, under the Pontificate of Boniface VIII.

FIFTEENTH CENTURY.

Gaetani Chapel in the Church of S. Pudentiana—SS. Praxedes and Pudentiana collecting the blood of the Martyrs with sponges. 3062

SIXTEENTH CENTURY.

S. CESAREO—On the vault of the Apse, A.D. 1592,
It represents the Almighty seated on a throne, His right hand raised giving the benediction, His left is resting on a globe supported by an

[c] An old French poet, very likely of the thirteenth century, represents S. Peter as having a black beard and twisted mustachios :

"Barbe et noire, grenons trechiez." (De Saint Pierre et du Jongleor, l. 132, in Fabliaux et contes, &c., t. iii. p. 286. Paris, MDCCCVIII. 8vo.)

angel ; another angel on His right hand is adoring. The whole are in theatrical attitudes.   1412

S. MARIA MAGGIORE. Restoration of two of the panels originally of the fifth century.

The Levites carrying the Ark of the Lord.   1413, 2059

Abraham going up the hill to sacrifice his son Isaac.   2060

SS. COSMAS AND DAMIAN, Figure of S. Felix, *as restored.*   797

Ara Cœli, over side door, Heads of the Madonna and two Saints, A. D. 1564.
                    2266

SEVENTEENTH CENTURY.

S. Paolo alle Tre Fontane, on the vault of a chapel in the Church of Scala Cœli—It represents the Virgin with four Saints, Clement VIII., and Cardinal Farnese.   3064

HISTORICAL PHOTOGRAPHS
ILLUSTRATIVE OF CHURCH AND ALTAR DECORATIONS.

[The numbers refer to Mr. Parker's Catalogue.]

COSMATI WORK.

SS. NEREO AND ACHILLEO.

Bishop's seat, Chair of S. Gregory. 310
Altar and Confessio, with perforated
  Marble Grille. 311
View of the Interior of the Church. 1172

S. CESAREO IN PALATIO.

View of the Interior of the Church, and
  Altar Canopy or Baldacchino, the
  Mosaic Picture, and the side Altars.
    1421
The Altar with the Confessio, under it
  the Cosmati work. 1407
The Cathedra or Bishop's seat, with
  the twisted Columns, &c. 1409
Choir-screen, with Panels of Porphyry
  and Cosmati work. 1408
Marble Pulpit of Cosmati work, of the
  thirteenth century, and made up again
  in the sixteenth. 1411
Side Altar, with Cosmati work, *restored.*
    1410

S. LORENZO OUTSIDE THE WALLS.

View of the Interior, shewing the general effect, with the Altar and its
  Canopy, the Pulpit, the Ambones or
  Reading-desk, the Choir-screen, and
  the Mosaic Pavement. 592

The Altar with its Canopy, *c.* A.D.
  1160. 593
The Ambo, and Paschal Candlestick.
    595
The Cathedra and Choir-screen, with
  Column, Panels of Porphyry, and
  Ribbon Mosaic. 596

S. GEORGIO IN VELABRO.

View of the Interior, shewing the Altar
  with its Canopy over it, and the
  Confessio under it. 1254
The Confessio separately, with the
  transenna or perforated marble, Mosaic Panels, and Ribbon Mosaic.
    1255

S. CLEMENT.

General View of the Interior, shewing
  the Altar. 1273
The Cathedra in the Apse. 1270
One of the Ambones, with the Paschal
  Candlestick. 1271
The Choir-screen, with the Monogram
  of Johannes. 1272

S. CECILIA IN TRASTEVERE.

View in the Interior, shewing the Altar
  with the elegant Gothic Canopy, the
  figure of the Saint under it, and the
  Apse. 1704

PAGAN REMAINS IN CHURCHES IN ROME.

THE PANTHEON,
S. Maria ad Martyres, called the Rotonda.

1. The Front, with the Portico added, and the Obelisk.   1350
3. Part of the Interior, shewing the Tomb of Raphael and the Altar of the Madonna del Sasso sculptured by him, and two of the Marble Columns of the original fabric.   732
4. The original Bronze Doors.   771
5. Cornice and Brickwork, and Window, of the time of Agrippa.   1237
2. View in the Interior, shewing the antique columns.   1648

TEMPLE OF BACCHUS (?),
S. Urban alla Caffarella.

View of the Front, with the Portico, *c.* A.D. 50.   1590
View of the Back, with the fine Brick Cornice of the first century.   1364
The Altar of Bacchus found there.   1365

TEMPLE OF ANTONINUS AND FAUSTINA, A.D. 138—161, S. Lorenzo in Miranda.

The Front, with the Portico.   298
Details—The Frieze, with beautiful Sculpture.   824
———— Construction of the Walls of Travertine.   975
———— Bases of the Column.   1220

TEMPLE OF FORTUNA VIRILIS,
S. Maria Egiziaca.

Side View (with the Medieval House near to it).   304
Construction of the Wall, of Travertine.   3053

TEMPLE OF VESTA (?), S. Maria del Sole.

TEMPLE OF ROMULUS, THE SON OF MAXENTIUS, &c., SS. Cosmas and Damian.

Front View of the round Temple.   268

Details—The Bronze Door and Porch, A.D. 820.   418
———— Doorway of the Temple of Roma (?), on the south side, excavated in 1868.   1135
———— Construction of it.   850
The same, from a drawing.   1137*
———— Wall on the east side of the Temple of Roma (?), to which the Marble Plan of Rome, A.D. 276, was attached.   783

TEMPLE OF MATER MATUTA (?), S. Maria in Cosmedin.

View of the Porch.   634
Details—Two Capitals (antique).   637
The "Bocca della Verita."   636
Plan.   344

TEMPLES OF SPES, JUNO SOSPITA, AND PIETAS,
now in S. Nicolas in Carcere.

Plan, shewing the foundation of the three Temples in the Crypt of the Church.   3200
Details of SPES.   261
Columns and Cornice, *from a drawing.*   663
Basement, *from a drawing.*   713
Construction of the Wall (*taken with magnesian light*).   1231
Construction of Wall, *from a drawing.*   718*
Of JUNO SOSPITA, Cornice.   1114
Column.   1112
Construction of Wall (*taken with magnesian light*).   1230

Of PIETAS, B.C. 180.
Cornice, with that of Spes, *from a drawing.*   666
———— ———— *from nature.*   1115
Construction of the Basement or Podium.   719
Wall in the foundation (*taken with magnesian light*).   1229
Fragments of the three Temples.   1117

TEMPLE OF JUPITER CAPITOLINUS (?),
S. Maria in Ara Cœli.
View of the Front, with the Marble
Steps. 583

TEMPLE OF SATURN (?), S. Hadrian
in the Forum.
General View. 306
Construction of the Wall. 998

TEMPLE OF JUNO (?),
S. Maria Maggiore.
General View of the Interior, with the
Marble Columns. 1454

TEMPLE OF DIANA,
S. Sabina.
View of the Interior. 323

THERMÆ OF HADRIAN,
SS. Silvester and Martinus.
Original Doorway, time of Trajan,
Construction. 1341
Plan of Subterranean Church. 227

THERMÆ OF DIOCLETIAN,
S. M. degli Angeli.
View of the Interior. 1586
View, shewing the Vault. 1587

S. BERNARD.
View of the Interior and the Vault. 1588

PORTA TRIUMPHALIS, in the Portico
or Colonnades of Octavia and Phi-
lippus, now S. Angelo in Peschiera.
1079
View in 1866, taken when the church
was rebuilding. 275
Plan, with the fragment of the Marble
Plan. 346
Details—Capitals of two Columns. 741

SARCOPHAGUS, with Sculpture of Apollo
and the Muses, now the Tomb of
Monsignor Spinelli, at the Priorato.
315
A Pagan Marriage ceremony—Cardinal
Fieschi at Ara Cœli. 597

PALACES AND HOUSES.
THERMÆ OF NOVATUS IN THE HOUSE
OF PUDENS,
S. Pudentiana.
Plan of the House, including the Thermæ
and the Church. 176
Plan of the Subterranean Chambers. 177
Wall behind the Altar, part of the
House, c. A.D. 20. 178
Chamber of the House, now subter-
ranean. 1733, 1734
Section of part of the House. 352
Section of the Viminal Hill, shewing
the site of the House. 148

HOUSE OF THE ANICIA FAMILY,
S. Gregorio al Monte Celio.
View of the Apse of the Hall or
Basilica. 996
Details—Marble Table. 217
Plan and View of the Ruins, with the
Monastery. 215, 216
View of the Ruins, *from a drawing*. 216

HOUSE OR PALACE OF PRISCILLA,
S. Prisca.
Font made of an antique Capital and
Base. 462
View in the Crypt or Subterranean
Chamber, *from a drawing*. 722
Plan of the Crypt or Subterranean
Chamber. 701

MAUSOLEUM OF S. HELENA,
SS. Peter and Marcellinus.
View of Exterior. 207
——— Interior. 208
Plan. 206

MAUSOLEUM AND BAPTISTERY NOW
CHURCH OF S. CONSTANTIA.
View of the Interior, shewing the
Twin-columns. 1600

MOSAIC PICTURES AT RAVENNA,
A.D. 550.
S. Vitale—Male Procession, with Justi-
nian and Maximianus. 752
——— Female Procession, with Theo-
dora and attendants. 753
——— Part of the Choir, with Arches
and Capitals covered with Mosaics.
754

HISTORICAL PHOTOGRAPHS OF
FRESCO PAINTINGS.

[*The numbers refer to Mr. Parker's Catalogue.*]

FIRST CENTURY.

HOUSE OF AUGUSTUS, on the Palatine, Mythological subjects and wall decorations in the state apartments, eight subjects. 2240 to 2248
On a vault in the Baths of Livia, on the Palatine. 2227
Pyramidal Tomb of CAIUS CESTIUS; in the chamber for the sarcophagus, two Genii of Death, each carrying a crown. 2982, 2983
Wall-painting in the Tomb of Hylas. 2653
Tomb in the Villa Pamphili-Doria, a series of wall-paintings between the rows of Columbaria, representing a Villa of the time of Augustus, with garden scenes, mythological subjects, birds and animals from a menagerie. Fourteen subjects, *taken with the magnesian light.* 2695 to 2708
House of Nero, taken from scarce engravings by De Romanis.
1879, 1880, 1887, 1888
(The originals are almost inaccessible, and much faded since his time.)

SECOND CENTURY.

Thermæ of Trajan on the Esquiline (excavated in 1873), the Rape of Europa and dancers. 3057,3058,3059
Private House of Trajan on the Aventine, a mythological subject on the wall of a chamber always subterranean (excavated in 1872). 2981
In the Private House of Hadrian, near the south end of the Thermæ of Caracalla (now in the Vigna Guidi), miscalled the Villa of Asinius Pollio. 1697, 1698, 1699
(These frescoes have now been

SECOND CENTURY.

almost destroyed by the great flood, since these photographs were taken.)
POMPEII. Several of the best frescoes, chiefly of mythological subjects, remaining on the walls in Pompeii, have been taken for comparison with Rome, and for illustrating the history of the Art of Drawing.
Seventeen subjects.
2170, 2176, 2177, 2178, 2179, 2180, 2182, 2186, 2187, 2188, 2189, 2190
Catacomb of the Jews on the Via Appia, in the Vigna Randanini. The curious paintings on the walls of a *cubiculum* (or burial vaulted chamber) in this catacomb are attributed to this period. There is a singular mixture of subjects, they are not distinctly Pagan, though they contain Pagan subjects, such as the Pegasus, nor is there anything distinctly Jewish nor Christian. They seem to be merely ornamental, and are very good drawing. *They have been taken with the magnesian light.*
561, 562, 773, 774, 775
An excellent drawing of this chamber has also been taken by Mr. Ewing, and is reproduced in No. 1161. No. 774 is a general view of the same from nature.
CATACOMB OF PRÆTEXTATUS. A painting representing the cultivation of the vine is attributed to this period, but may be later. 615 and 1822

THIRD CENTURY.

STADIUM ON THE PALATINE. Figures on the wall of the Exhedra.
2302, 2303

THIRD CENTURY.

In the Tomb of the Gordiani, A.D. 240.   923

Catacomb of S. Domitilla, the allegorical figures of the four seasons, with their usual emblems and attendant genii, are probably of this century.

618, 619, 1820

Considerable importance is attached by one party to a small painting in the Catacomb of S. Priscilla attributed to this century, said to represent the Madonna, with the star of Bethlehem over her head, addressed by a figure said to be a prophet, called by some the Prophet of Bethlehem, by others S. Joseph. The painting is in a very bad state, and the date cannot be relied on. If the original, taken with the magnesian light, No. 1467, is compared with the drawings of it usually published, it will be seen that little reliance can be placed on them. The subject of the Seasons is also found in S. Calixtus (Nos. 1808, 1809), but appears to belong to a later period, more likely the fifth century than the third.

FOURTH CENTURY.

There are numerous frescoes of this period in the Catacombs, but they are always of Scriptural subjects ; no figure of a saint or martyr, not Scriptural, is of an earlier period than the sixth century. Those in S. Calixtus, in the chapel of the Sacraments, were probably of this period, though now touched up and *restored:* An Agape (1804) ; Christ and the Woman of Samaria? (1801); Abraham and Isaac and a fossor (1806) ; Christ after His Resurrection, with fish and bread upon a tripod, and a female figure, probably the Church (1805).

The very curious paintings of the mysteries of the worship of Mithra (commonly called the Gnostic paintings), in part of the great Catacomb of the family of Prætextatus, are probably of this century, *or later.*

1281, 1791, 1792, 1793, 1794

FIFTH CENTURY.

The most favourite subject of the Catacomb pictures of this period is the history of Jonah, sometimes with the whale or sea-serpent, as in S. Calixtus.   1802

SIXTH CENTURY.

The Madonna in the corridor for the Sentinels, in the Wall of Aurelian. The painting is believed to be of the time of Belisarius, A.D. 538. No.1208

Several paintings in the catacombs of S. Priscilla, SS. Saturninus and Thrason, SS. Nereus and Achilleus, and Domitilla, are of the time of Pope John I., A.D. 523, as recorded in the Pontifical Registers published by Anastasius the librarian.

S. Priscilla.

612, 1468, 1469, 1470, 1471, 1472

S. Domitilla.   465, 466

SS. Nereus and Achilleus.

1609, 1612, 1613, 1614, 1615, 1616

SS. Saturninus and Thrason.

475, 476, 480, 1752

Catacomb of Generosa, Head of Christ.

1159

EIGHTH CENTURY.

Catacombs of SS. Saturninus and Thrason. These adjoin to those of S. Priscilla, and many of the paintings in the cubicula or burial-vaults, and in the corridors or passages, were restored by the Popes in the eighth and ninth centuries, after they had been much damaged by the Lombards during the siege of Rome. These restorations are recorded in the Pontifical Registers of Pope Hadrian I., A.D. 772—795. Nos. 1751, 1774, 1775, 1776, 1777, 1778, 1779

—— SS. Peter and Marcellinus, Christ and two Apostles (No. 2119) ; Agape (No. 2117, 2118) ; Madonna and the Magi (No. 2116) ; A female Orante, with two other female figures addressing her.   2115

—— SS. Nereus and Achilleus, an Orante, with a sheep.   1816

—— S. Agnes.   627

—— Naples, the figures of SS. Desiderius and Agutius are of this period

EIGHTH CENTURY.

(No. 2148). Several other frescoes in this catacomb are most probably also of this time.

2146, 2149, 2150, 2151

Oratory of S. Silvester, in the church of the Santi Quattri Coronati; the life of Constantine represented in a series of paintings on the walls of this chapel, in six panels.

2214 to 2219

Church of S. Cæcilia. The finding and deposition of the body of the Saint, represented in a painting said to be of this period. 1861

—— S. Clement. The descent of Christ into Hades. 2647, 2648

Christ and Saints. 2649, 2651

—— S. Clement in the crypt, a group of heads of nuns. 1415

—— S. Urban in the crypt. The Madonna with Christ as a child; S. Urban and S. John, *c.* A.D. 817. 1371

—— S. Prassede, in the chapel of S. Anne. The legend of that Saint (much faded). 1505

NINTH CENTURY.

Catacombs of S. Pontianus. The frescoes on this catacomb are in a better state of preservation than any of the others, but this belongs almost entirely to the Restoration of Pope Nicolas I. (A.D. 858–867); they include some of the most celebrated paintings in the Catacombs. A fine head of Christ (No. 607 A), which has been frequently published from drawings, which are intended to be *improvements* of the originals, but lose their authenticity. 463, 607 B

The Baptism of Christ (No. 608), also frequently published from drawings (No. 608 B); and the Jewelled Cross (No. 609 A), also reproduced from a drawing (No. 609 B). Figures of SS. Marcellinus, Pollion, and Petrus (No. 610 A), reproduced (610 B).

Catacomb of S. Calixtus. The paintings

NINTH CENTURY.

in a part of this catacomb are also of this period, such as the figure of S. Cæcilia, of Christ, and of S. Urban (No. 1800); S. Cornelius, M. (No. 1813); S. Xystus, Pope, and S. Optatus (No. 1814).

Church of S. Clement in the crypt. The Madonna in the Byzantine style, A.D. 858—867. 1267

ILLUMINATIONS and Initial Letters from the Manuscript of the Bible, given by Charles the Bald to the Monastery of S. Paul, f.m. Rome, A.D. 850. Twenty-eight subjects.

3090 to 3114

ELEVENTH CENTURY.

Church of S. Urban. Paintings for the pilgrims by Benizzo, A.D. 1001, on the side walls; those on the two ends have been *restored*, these are genuine; the Nativity, the Raising of Lazarus, and the Crucifixion.

1366, 1367, 1368, 1369

Church of S. Clement in the crypt. The Crucifixion and the Resurrection, A.D. 1049—1055. 1269

———— The Ascension of Christ in the presence of the Apostles, with figures of S. Vitus, Abp. of Verona, and of Pope Leo IX., A.D. 1049—1055. 1268

Church of S. Clement, originally in the nave, now made the crypt, by raising the floor. A fine series of paintings by Beno de Rapiza, *c.* A.D. 1080, representing the legends of S. Alexius and S. Clement, *taken with the magnesian light.* 1264, 1265, 1266, 2650

—— Workmen dragging a column. 2650

—— The Funeral of S. Cyril, and the funeral procession. 1461

—— Head of Christ, and under it figures of Beno de Rapiza, his wife, and son. 1420

N.B. These remarkable paintings, now taken from the originals by photography, should be compared with the fine set made from drawings sold in the sacristy.

TWELFTH CENTURY.

Church of S. Prassede, in the crypt, over the altar, the Blessed Virgin, with SS. Prassede and Pudentiana, *c.* A. D. 1200, *taken with the magnesian light.* 1370
—— *the same, from a drawing.* 473
—— S. Maria in Cosmedin, Saints. 1874

THIRTEENTH CENTURY.

Church of S. John Lateran. Head of Christ (now in the cloisters). 1731
—— S. Lorenzo, outside the walls. A series of fresco pictures of the legend of that saint, A. D. 1216, *restored,* but the old drawing preserved. Seven subjects. 1120 to 1126

FOURTEENTH CENTURY.

Church of S. Paul, outside the walls. A series of fresco paintings of Scriptural subjects of this period, from the old church, have been preserved in the passage leading to the cloisters. Seven subjects. 2024 to 2030
Crypt of S. Peter's in the Vatican. A Madonna, with Christ as a youth, and two attendant angels. 2984

FIFTEENTH CENTURY.

Church of S. John Lateran. A fresco painting of the Madonna is preserved in the cloister. 1730
—— S. Maria del Popolo. A Madonna, now in the sacristy. 2279

FIFTEENTH CENTURY.

Church of S. Clement. Legend of S. Catherine by Masaccio, *c.* A. D. 1440, in her chapel near the door of this church. 1425
Crypt of S. Peter's in the Vatican. View of the interior of the old church of S. Peter. 2988
Castle of S. Angelo, in an external loggia. Two views of the Mausoleum of Hadrian, as then proposed to be restored ; and of the Cupola or Dome of S. Peter's Church, as then proposed. 3006, 3007

SIXTEENTH CENTURY.

Church of Ara Cœli. Two frescoes by Pinturiccio, of Christ and S. Bernard (No. 2271), and the Death of S. Bernard. 2270
Castle of S. Angelo. A series of fine Fresco Paintings on the walls of the Great Hall of the Popes over the Mausoleum of Hadrian, the work of the pupils of Raphael, as under :—
—— Scenes in the life of Alexander the Great and King Pyrrhus, by Siciolante, A. D. 1504.
3008, 3009, 3010, 3011, 3012
—— Historical and Mythological subjects, by Pierino del Vago.
3013, 3014, 3023, 3024, 3025
—— By Giulio Romano, A. D. 1540. Eight subjects. 3015 to 3022

THE ART OF SCULPTURE.

[*The numbers refer to Mr. Parker's Catalogue.*]

OUR collection of photographs illustrating the History of Sculpture is so large that it is difficult to arrange it in such a manner as to be clear and easy for reference. In the Numerical Catalogue (which is made chiefly for the use of the photographers, and to serve for lettering-pieces to each photograph), they are arranged in the order in which they were taken, or nearly as they stand in the different museums in Rome, the Vatican, the Lateran, the Capitoline, and the Villa Albani. This is the most convenient arrangement for persons on the spot, or for those who are well acquainted with these great Museums, and the numbers of each Museum are also retained. It is also convenient for public libraries, for comparison with the outline engravings in the great folio works on the subject, entitled "IL VATICANO," and "IL CAMPIDOGLIO." WINCKELMANN formed and illustrated the collection now in the "Villa Albani," and he would gladly have availed himself of photography to illustrate his history of sculpture, if it had then been invented. Our photographs are intended to be supplementary to these great works as more convenient for reference, and for the use of those who have not access to them. It seems, however, useless to repeat the catalogue in this form, as it is to be had, and the numbers make reference to it very easy; but an indication of the various subjects illustrated, with references to the numbers, was required, and is here given, arranged as nearly as possible in the same order as in our chapter on the subject, and adding the numbers.

VIEWS IN THE MUSEUMS.

Vatican Museum.

Views in different compartments and galleries, or corridors, and halls.
2417, 2446, 2447, 2514, 2515, 2537, 2607, 2612

Villa Albani, now Torlonia.

General View of the Palace.	2749
View of the Gardens.	2750
View of one of the side Entrances.	2751

View on the Capitol, shewing the situation of the Museum, with one of the Trophies of Marius and the Statues of Castor and Marcus Aurelius, and of Pollux. 1649, 1650

—— Another view with Pallas, called Roma Trionfante, and the Statues of the Tiber and the Nile, at the Fountain. 1651

Capitoline Museums.

Portrait Busts of the Emperors.

A Series of eighty-three Busts of the Emperors and Empresses, from Julius Cæsar, B.C. 49, to Julian the Apostate, A.D. 360, arranged in chronological order, taken in a set of eight photographs. 1660 to 1667
This series is very useful for shewing the succession of costume or the mode of wearing the hair and the beard at each period, and they also are authentic portraits for comparison.
In front of No. 1667 is a statue of Agrippina seated.

First Century.

The young Augustus.	2432
Augustus, a colossal head.	331
Claudius, crowned with oak-leaves.	2601
Nero, a colossal head, with the Agonistic crown.	2534
Titus (colossal).	2794
Domitian (colossal).	87

Trajan (colossal).	2488, 2795
Plotina, the wife of Trajan.	2608

Centuries II. and III.

Hadrian, on the Basis Capitolina.	1694
—— Colossal.	2593
Marcus Antoninus.	2471
Marcus Aurelius.	2772
Lucius Verus.	2770
Commodus.	2479
Pertinax.	2606
Didius Julianus (?).	2452
Julia Domna, second wife of Septimius Severus.	2604

Historical Busts—Roman.

Numa, dressed as a priest.	2776
Pompey the Great.	337
Brutus.	1682
Caius Marius (?).	2436
M. E. Lepidus.	2472
Quintus Hortensius.	2822
The celebrated Colonna Rostrale of Caius Duillius, now in the Palazzo de' Conservatori on the Capitol.	1657

PORTRAIT STATUES OF THE
EMPERORS, &c.

Julius Cæsar (the only genuine statue
of him). 1655
Augustus. 1089, 1656, 2769
The Genius of Augustus. 2605
Livia Drusilla, fourth wife of Augustus.
2540
Marcellus (?), nephew of Augustus. 2635
Tiberius. 2436, 2764, 2874
Caligula. 2527
Claudius. 2412, 2600
Titus. 2456
Julia, daughter of Titus. 2474
Domitian. 2483
Nerva. 2454, 2598
Trajan. 2766
Hadrian. 2768
Sabina, wife of Hadrian. 2438
Antoninus Pius. 2767
Lucius Verus. 2480, 2552, 2765
Commodus. 2449, 2509
Claudius Albinus. 2516
Geta, son of Septimius Severus. 2790
Opimius Macrinus. 2543

M. Junius Brutus. . 2763
Marcus Marcellus. 1007

PORTRAIT STATUES—GREEK.

Lycurgus. 2587
Sappho, the Poetess. 2810
Sophocles. 2876
Demosthenes. 2464
Menander, seated. 2541
King Pyrrhus, or Mars Cyprius, with
rich armour. 851
Posidippus, seated. 2533
Pancratiastes, or Gimnasiargus. 843

PORTRAIT HERMES
AND BUSTS — GREEK.

(N.B. Hermes is a technical name
for a head, or a head and bust, on the
top of a short square column, much
used in gardens ; there are frequently
two faces or masks, then called also
Janus.) 1328

Menelaus. 2535
Homer. 2807
Sappho, the Poetess. 2847
Demosthenes. 2433
Epimenides. 2582
(He is said to have slept for forty
years continually.)
Zeno, the Epicurean. 2583
Periander. 2581, 2587
Æsop, a fragment (the only portrait of
him known). 2824
Bias, the Sage. 2579, 2587
Themistocles. 2580
Socrates. 2849
Pericles. 2585
Alcibiades. 2434
Aspasia, of Miletus. 2586
Isocrates, the orator. 2820
Corinna (?). 2778
Aristotle. 2441
Theophrastus. 2848
Epicurus. 2578
Euripides. 2584
A Philosopher (?). 2774

STATUES
OF GODS AND GODDESSES.

Jupiter, or Jove. 2538, 2844, 2793
APOLLO. 1677, 2503, 2528, 2560,
2571, 2777, 2796, 2816, 2821
Mars. 2870
Neptune. 2878
Oceanus, or Marforio. 1668
The Nile. 2473
Silenus. 2437, 2566
Silenus and Bacchus. 2451
BACCHUS. 2524, 2620, 2779, 2811
A Faun, with the Infant Bacchus.
2622, 2755
Torso of Bacchus. 2551
MERCURY. 2443, 2484, 2496, 2553, 2623
Cupid. 1674, 2435, 2518
Cupid on a Dolphin. 2884
Cupid and Psyche. 2743
Harpocrates. • 1185
Æsculapius and Hygeia. 2544
Æsculapius. 338, 2453, 2867
Priapus. 3498
Somnus, or Sleep. 2621

E 2

HERCULES as a child. 1232, 2965
—— with his club. 1154, 2818
—— colossal figure in bronze. 2594
—— in Greek marble. 2809
—— the Belvidere Torso. 2485
—— Torso of Hercules, in the Thermæ
of Caracalla. 2735, 2736, 2737
Juno, 2771 ; Juno Regina, 2596 ; Juno
Sospita, 2602
Pallas, or Minerva.
2476, 2819, 2826, 2840
Ceres. 2467, 2592, 2639, 2752
Tellus, or The Earth. 2966
Diana of Ephesus. 2616, 2802
DIANA. 2420, 2463, 2633
Diana the Huntress. 1168, 2797
Diana Lucifera. 2440, 2557
Diana Triformis. 2424
VENUS. 2744, 2745, 2760, 2808
Venus after the Bath. 2555, 2556
Venus Anadyome. 2428, 2469
Venus Genetrix. 2754
The Venus of Guido. 2609

Isis. 2753
Flora. 2433
Fortune. 2468
Innocence. 2748
Modesty. 2063, 2455
Winter. 2418
City of Antioch. 2699

BUSTS OF THE GODS AND
GODDESSES.
Saturn. 2536, 2629
Jupiter. 1501, 2590
—— Serapis. 2599, 2803
—— Ammon. 2539
Vulcan. 2433
Oceanus. 2427
Neptune. 2444
A Marine God. 2597
Dionysius, or The Bearded Bacchus.
1395, 2421
Juno Regina. 2475
Pallas. 2425
Venus. 2436
Isis. 2439
Medusa. 2470
Ceres. 1501
Cybele. 1501

STATUES OF FAUNS, MUSES,
HEROES, &c.

FAUNS. 1679, 1680, 2817, 2823
—— of Praxiteles. 2478, 2871
—— playing on a pipe, 2460 ; dancing,
2875; drunken, 2531 ; reclining, 2459
—— a Satyr extracting a thorn. 2615
A Satyr and Child. 2873
—— playing a pipe. 2834
A Bacchante dancing. 2521, 2554, 2773
A Triton. 2520
A Nymph. 2490, 2805
—— on a sea monster. 2780, 2783
A Triton carrying off a Nymph. 2512
A Hippocampus, or Marine Horse, with
a Nereid on his back. 2457, 2458
A Centaur. 1044, 1236

STATUES OF THE MUSES, &c.

Calliope. 2571
Clio, Urania, and Thalia. 2576
Clio, or History. 2419
Erato dancing. 2570
Terpsichore. 2571, 2699
Euterpe. 2572
Urania, or Astronomy. 2575
Polyhymnia, or Memory, &c. 2577
Melpomene, or Tragedy. 2573
Thalia, or Comedy. 2574, 2761
Tuccia Vestalis. 338
The Vestal Virgin Luccia. 2445
A Canephora, with her basket (?) on
her head. 2756, 2759

BUSTS OF THE MUSES.
Muse of Comedy. 2589
Muse of Tragedy. 2588

STATUES OF HEROES, &c.
Perseus. 2491
Theseus and the Minotaur. 2786
Meleager. 2487
Paris. 2522
Ganymede. 2599
Ganymede and the Eagle. 2656
Antinous. 1676
—— (colossal). 2591, 2868
Marsyas, punished by Apollo. 2799

Ariadne abandoned by Theseus. 1090
Dido meditating. 2542
Penelope. 2526
Leda and the Swan. 2785
One of the Danaids. 2545
One of the daughters of Niobe. 2422
THE CELEBRATED LAOCOON. 2501
The Mithraic Sacrifice. 2507, 2657
Victory sacrificing a Bull. 2657
An Hermaphrodite. 2791
Gladiators. 2492, 2493
The dying Gladiator. 1678
Athletes. 2465, 2762
Amazons. 1675, 2461, 2466, 2529
The Discobulus. 2481, 2611
A Spartan Virgin. 2636
Barbarian Prisoners. 93, 2429, 2892
Comic Statue of a Shepherd. 2800
An Actor in a Mask. 2637
A Præfica in tears. 2442
Female Statues, time of the Flavian
  Emperors. 2499
An old Fisherman. 2627
A Hunter. 1185
A Warrior. 2638
A Priest, 2829; and a Priestess (Ar-
  chaic style), 2831.
A Priest of Mithra. 2558
Caryatides. 2448, 2462, 2757, 2798
An unknown Person, nude. 2789
A Child playing with a Goose. 1262
A Child with a Swan. 2630, 2631
Statues of Children. 2430, 2613, 2639

BUSTS OF HEROES, &c.

Antinous (colossal). 2595
The Minotaur (colossal). 2513
Arianna (crowned with ivy). 1685
Dacian Prisoners, or Slaves.
  2450, 2477, 2482
Busts of Females. 2434, 2436
A Janus, or head with two faces. 1328

STATUES—EGYPTIAN.

An Egyptian Statue, with a figure of
  Isis, front. 1789
—— back, with a long Inscription.
  1788

STATUES—ETRUSCAN.

Marzio Pastore (?). 1681
  A youth drawing a thorn from his
  foot.
An Etruscan Soldier, or Pioneer.
  2721, 2722
  (The front and back of the same
  figure; he carries a hand-barrow on
  his shoulders, which stands up over
  his head.)
ANIMALS.

The celebrated Etruscan bronze Wolf,
  B.C. 296, with Romulus and Remus
  added. 1659
A colossal Bronze Horse. 1699
A Biga with two Horses. 293
A Monkey with a Cocoa-nut. 2511
A Stag, with a Hound on his back.
  2504, 2510
Two Greyhounds, one licking the ear
  of the other. 2506
A Lion upon a Horse. 90
Heads of Animals, Camels (?), &c.,
  from the Temple of Trajan. 814

COLOSSI AND FRAGMENTS.

The Colossal Horses, with the Statues
  of Castor and Pollux, the work of
  Phidias and Praxiteles, (now in the
  Piazza di Monte Cavallo). 1087
Colossal Hand. 86
—— Foot. 89
—— Arm. 92
—— Foot, called Piè di Marmo. 1332
Fragments of Colossal Statues.
  1653, 1654

MISCELLANEOUS FRAGMENTS.
Fragments of a Statue in the Thermæ
  of Caracalla. 1071
Fragment of a Statue in drapery (ad-
  mired by Raphael). 2486
Fragments of Sculpture, and View of
  the Exedra of a Palace. 2239
Fragments found on the Palatine, now
  in the Museum there. 2292, 2293
Fragments of Sculpture found in the
  Forum. 2732
Fragments of ancient Sculpture, with
  the arms of the Colonna family,
  A.D. 1500. 1249
Inscriptions and Fragments of Sculp-
  ture, from the Tomb of Hylas. 2654

SCULPTURE IN PANELS
in Bas-relief.

MYTHOLOGICAL SUBJECTS.

NEPTUNE.

Neptune in the Archaic style. 2564

BACCHUS.

Leucothea and Bacchus. 2828
A female figure in a chair with
a child.
Birth of Bacchus. (Greek Style.)
(Cent. I.) 2567
Infancy of Bacchus of the first century,
a Nymph gives him drink. 1492
A Feast of Bacchus. (Cent. II.) 2547
Bacchus and Hercules seated in the
same car. (Cent. II.) 2563
Bacchus, the Conqueror of the Indies,
addressed by a Female figure repre-
senting the East. 2784
A Bacchante, in Greek marble 2835

HERCULES.

Contest of Apollo with Hercules for
the Tripod of Delphi. 2827
(Under it an Etruscan Cinerary Urn
of Alabaster, with a Figure reclining
on the cover.)
The Labours of Hercules. 2885
Hercules in the Gardens of the Hes-
perides. 2836
Tripod representing the Combat of
Hercules with the sons of Hippo-
dorus. 295

VARIOUS SUBJECTS.

Theseus and Ariadne. 2626
Death of the Sons of Niobe. 2812
Perseus delivering Andromeda from
the Sea-monster. 2746
Ariadne abandoned by Theseus, on one
side Bacchus, and a Bacchante on
the other. 2550
Ganymede and the Eagle. 2839
Dædalus making the wings for Icarus.
2837
Endymion with his Dog. 2747
Mars and Rea Silvia. 2562

Orestes and Pylades recognised by the
Priestess Iphigenia. 2787
Philocletes wounded in the Isle of
Lemnos. 1491
The Cyclop Polyphemus seated, while
a Cupid at the back induces him to
sing. 2782
Æsculapius and Hygeia with the two
Dioscuri. Greek art. 2525
Antiope with Zethus and Amphion.
2846

NYMPHS.

A Donation to the Nymphs, with an
Archaic Inscription of the Family
of Alcibiades. (Cent. II.) 2565
Two Nymphs dancing. 2825

SACRIFICES, &c.

A Mithraic Sacrifice ; under it a Nymph
on a Sea-monster. 2780
A Sacrifice. 2842, 2546, 2838
Altar, representing the Statue of Cy-
bele in a Boat, drawn by the Vestal
Virgin Salvia, with Inscription. 1027
Two celebrated Bas-reliefs. 840
One representing an Archigalles,
or chief-priest of Cybele, with all the
attributes and symbols of this god-
dess, discovered at Civita Lavinia.
The other a Palmyran monument,
dedicated to Aglibolus and Malach-
beles, gods of Palmyra, by Marcus
Aurelius Æliodorus, with a Greek
and Palmyran inscription, with a
Latin translation.
Cybele and Atys. 2788
A Priestess before a Divinity. 2832
A Procession in honour of Isis, 2497
Two Female Figures going to fulfil
a religious ceremony. 2845

LEAVE-TAKING BEFORE DEATH.

A scene of leave-taking before death.
(Cent. I.) Greek. 2532
(The serpent round the tree is a
symbol of the deceased.)
A Greek Funeral, representing a leave-
taking between a soldier and his wife
2853

HISTORICAL SUBJECTS.

Diogenes in his Tub conversing with Alexander the Great ; under it a Nymph on a Sea-monster.   2783

Pollux dismounted from his Horse to fight with Lynceus.   2830

The Wolf, with the infants Romulus and Remus, in the cave of the Palatine, called the Lupercal.   2561.

Temple of Romulus.   2283

(On the frontal the story of the birth of Romulus and Remus is represented. It is considered an important piece of sculpture, and is engraved in Canina's work. The representation agrees with a coin of the Temple of Venus and Roma.)

The celebrated Bas-relief of Metius Curtius, found under the Church of S. Maria Liberatrice, near the Forum Romanum.   1658

(Metius Curtius is represented plunging himself and his horse into the gulf that opened between the Palatine and the Capitol.)

Trajan, followed by the Lictors, with book in his hand.   1496

FROM THE ARCH OF MARCUS AURELIUS.

The Apotheosis of Faustina, the wife of Marcus Aurelius.   1686

Marcus Aurelius in the Triumphal Quadriga.   1687

Rome consigning the empire of the world to Marcus Aurelius.   1688

Marcus Aurelius sacrificing.   1689

Marcus Aurelius granting peace to the Germans.   1690

M. Aurelius, Faustina and Roma. 2843

Rome seated on the spoils of the conquered nations.   5755

(This bas-relief is attributed to the time of the Flavian Emperors. The Temple in the background is modern.)

Sculptures from the Marble Walls of the COMITIUM, found in the Forum Romanum in 1872. 2960, 2961, 2962

The Emperor Septimius Severus and his wife, Julia Pia, with a Sacrifice, and the instruments of sacrifice, from the smaller Arch of Septimius Severus, built by the Silversmiths.   772

Column of Antoninus Pius, A.D. 160, Base, with Sculpture of a Military Funeral Procession.   327, 328

Column of Antoninus Pius, A.D. 160, Base, representing the Apotheosis of Antoninus and Faustina.   329

Details of Sculpture from Trajan's Column.   811, 812

Capaneus, on the base of the Caryatid ; he is believed by Winckelmann to have been one of the seven heroes of the expedition against Thebes. 2758

The celebrated Antinous crowned with Lotus flowers.   2833 A & B

(This bas-relief is considered the finest sculpture of the Albani collection.)

Antinous represented as one of the Castors.   2841

Cosmo I., Duke of Tuscany, in the act of improving the City of Pisa by driving away the Vices and introducing the Virtues and Sciences ; said to be by Michael Angelo.   2517

MASKS.

A Comic Actor near a Table, to whom a Youth is presenting a Mask. 2815

A Shop for Masks.   2877

CHARIOT-RACE.

A Chariot-race with the Meta, the Carceres, and the Obelisk.   2856

A Quadrigus on the Arch of Constantine, of the time of Trajan.   823

VARIOUS SUBJECTS.

Boxers, in high-relief, called Dares and Entellus.   2854

A Gallic or German prisoner (the head and the shoulders restored).   2610

The Personification of a Mountain. 2813

Fragment, ornamented with Sculptures and Bas-reliefs.   2792

A Sculptor taking the Portrait of a Woman. (Cent. II.)   2624

Base, with a Foot, said to belong to a Statue of Venus found near S. Cesareo, with very fine Bas-reliefs representing marine subjects.   2742

Apollo, on a panel in basso relievo (first century), standing on a fine antique base in the Thermæ of Titus.   1867

Ceres (first century), standing on a fine antique base.   1868

A Priest (first century), standing on a fine antique base.   1869

Military Figure by the side of a horse.   2781

(Peculiar from its having a wood represented in the background.)

Fragment of a Greek Bas-relief of very good style, similar to that of the Frieze of the Parthenon in Athens.   2430

It was formerly in the Palazzo Giustiniani, and is no doubt from Greece.

Door of a Temple, with Genii.   1672

A Genius of Death in front of a Tomb.   2814

BAS-RELIEFS FROM TOMBS.

THE TOMB OF THE ATERII, first century. A temple, or a tomb, and a machine for raising stones and a ladder, by means of a treadmill, mentioned by Vitruvius.   1500

(It seems probable that this was the tomb of an architect, (see the "Annali dell' Instituto di Corrispondenza Archeologica, 1849," and the "Building News," London, 1872.)

———— The Arcus in Sacra Via Summa, Arcus ad Isis, and the Temple —of Jupiter Stator(?).   1501

———— The defunct in his bed surrounded by torches; in the lower one, other funeral ceremonies.   2883

Tomb, with busts of the deceased of the time of Augustus.   1491

Busts of the Cavia Family.   1748

Tomb of Statilius Aper, Measurer of Buildings, with his Portrait and a wild Boar (*aper*) to shew the origin of his name.   1021

Funeral Cippus (Inferior Style) representing a soldier, of the third century.   2409

(The stick he holds in his left hand shews that he was a Centurion.)

Left-hand side of the Tomb of L. Cornelius Atimetus and L. Cornelius Epaphras, Cutlers, representing a shop-front. (Cent. I.)   2406

A cippus with the figure of a youth called SULPICIUS MAXIMUS attired in toga, with two long inscriptions, one on either side of the niche, consisting of a prize poem in forty-three hexameter verses, which he had *improvised* at eleven years of age, in the Capitoline competition, in the time of Domitian. Beneath is his epitaph in Latin, and two Greek epigrams composed in his honour.   2070

MISCELLANEOUS.

Curious Medieval Sculpture in bas-relief of the Porta Asinaria and the ancient Lateran.   1726

Consular Fasces in the Capitoline Museum.   1040

Roman Eagle, found in the Forum of Cæsar.   1652

Arms of the Roman Senate, from the Tomb of Agrippina.   91

An Argolic Buckler, with a border of flowers on the sides; above is a hunt, with animals in a garden, with its enclosure.   337

Altar of the second century, on a Terrace of the Capitoline Hill, above the Tarpeian Rock.   588

Bas-relief with beautiful Ornaments; under it Cybele and Atys.   2788

Bas-relief with Foliage and two Genii, partly restored.   2801

Fragments of Bas-reliefs built into the wall of the Villa Campana. 1944

Bas-relief of a Lion upon a Bull at the corner of the Piazza dell' Orso. 1391

Mascherone(?), a Mask or Head, with bands, in the Vicolo dè Vecchiarelli. 1457

Lion's Head, of the third century, built into a house, at the corner of the Vicolo del Falcone. 1446

A modern basso-relievo on the Pincian, by Ciccarini, in the time of Pius VII. 2061

Victory in the act of crowning the genii of terrestrial and of naval war, in imitation of the antique.

ALTARS.

Altar, with a Bas-relief of the Sacrifice of Mithra, found, and preserved in the lower Church or Crypt of S. Clement. 1426

VASES, CANDELABRI, &c.

ORNAMENTED WITH BAS-RELIEFS.

A Vase in the Garden of the Villa Campana, ornamented with Bas-reliefs. 1943

Basin of a fountain. 2617, 2618

Vase, ornamented with Bas-reliefs. 1943

Antique Vase (*dolium*) placed upon a Base, in which antique basso-relievi are inserted. 2065

Marble Vase with Bas-reliefs representing Lycurgus, king of Thrace, in the act of violating the sacred feasts of Bacchus. 2614

Antique Vase, representing a Feast of Bacchus. (Cent. I.) 2628

Vase, with Bas-reliefs, representing the Genii of Bacchus. 2640

Vase, with Bas-reliefs, representing Neptune between two Sea-monsters. 2632

One of the very fine Candelabra called the "Candelabri Barberini." 2548, 2549, 2625, 2881

Cinerary Urn of Luccia Telesina, richly ornamented. 2264

Cinerary Urn of Europus. 2502

Cinerary Urn of the Liberta Plutia Hygia. 2502

Etruscan Cinerary Urn in Alabaster. 2827

Cinerary Urn, with inscription. 2659

Stone Coffer, or Ossuarium, made as a Model of a small Temple, *c.* A.D. 350. . 296

SCULPTURE ON PAGAN SARCOPHAGI.

MYTHOLOGICAL SUBJECTS.

BACCHUS and Bacchanalian Scenes. 1038, 1043, 2423, 2489, 2530, 2828, 2886, 2890

Bacchus and Ariadne. 2550

HUNTING-SCENES.

The Caledonian Boar, Venus and Adonis. 894, 1359, 2858, 2888, 2889, 3047, 3048

BATTLE-SCENES, &c.

Romans and Barbarians. 1683, 2494

Theseus and Athenians and Amazons. 351, 1050, 2495, 2500

Centaurs and Lapithæ. 2568

Centaurs and Fauns. 2569

Giants and Gods 1090, 2494

Fable of Laodamia and Protesilaus. 2619

Death of the Niobides. 2634

Rape of Proserpine. 1051, 2519

Castor and Pollux carrying off the daughters of Lysippus. 2638

Rhæa Sylvia. 2857

Diana and Endymion. 838, 1041, 2523, 2639, 2857

CIRCENSIAN GAMES—CHARIOT RACES, &c. 290, 291, 292, 339, 2658, 2856

Athletes. 2869

Sarcophagus, with figures of Actors and Masks. 2980

NYMPHS?

Tritons and Nymphs. 85, 2415, 2502, 2894

Various Subjects.

A Nuptial Ceremony. 597

A Seaport—Carthage (?). 335

A Ship drawn by horses along a canal. 2112

An early Chariot, with men, horses, and dogs. 330

A Miller and a horse-mill. 294

Sarcophagi of known Persons.

P. Cornelius Scipio Barbatus, B.C. 298. 336

T. Paconius Calendus and his wife Octavia Salvia. (Cent. II.) 2404

Publius Nonius Zethus, a miller at Ostia, *c.* A.D. 200. 338

(This sculpture stands between the figures of Esculapius and Tuccia Vestalis, shewn in the photograph.)

Alexander Severus and his mother Mammea (?). 1673

(This is very doubtful; the figures on the top do not agree with the statues of these persons.)

P. Cæcilius Vallianus. 2891

(The defunct is represented in his bed, surrounded by his servants.)

Sextus Varius Marcellus. 2490

(He was the father of the Emperor Heliogabalus: there is an inscription on the tomb, in Greek and Latin.)

Sarcophagi, with Portraits of the Deceased.

Third Century.

A Youth surrounded by Genii. Behind this Sarcophagus is the statue of a Child in the act of playing.

The deceased amidst the four Seasons. (Cent. III.) 2499

Over it is a female statue of the time of the Flavian Emperors; this cover belonged formerly to another Sarcophagus.

Portrait of the defunct, with a roll of parchment at his feet, and another in his hand, which seems to shew he was an orator. Around him are two female and three male figures, perhaps members of his family. 2855

Portrait of the deceased surrounded by Minerva and the Muses. 315

(Now the Tomb of Monsignor Spinelli in the Church of the Priorato on the Aventine.)

Large Sarcophagus found at Roma Vecchia. 2408

In the centre is the door of the Tomb, with the figures of a husband and wife. (Cent. II.)

Genii of Death, and the Portraits of the deceased in the Niches, *c.* A.D. 200. 332

Portraits of the deceased, and two Muses, *c.* A.D. 250. 333

Five Figures in niches. (Cent. III.) 2111

The figures represent the family interred, the father and mother seated at the two extremities, and the children between them.

Half-Front of a Sarcophagus. 2872

On the right, the defunct asleep; on the left, the same in the act of sacrificing. On the frieze, children playing with two cocks and flowers.

Portraits of the Family, in Niches formed of Columns and Entablatures, *c.* A.D. 300. 334

Of the Fourth Century.

Sarcophagus with Sculpture unfinished, with fragments of the marble ornaments of a Temple, &c. 1228

—— Now a Fountain, near the Church of S. Maria del Popolo. 1363

Church of S. Clement—Crypt. 1280

The Sarcophagus in the crypt of the church of S. Clement appears to be of the fourth century, with uncommon carving; a head in the centre, and on either side festoons.

PAINTED TOMBS ON THE VIA LATINA —Sarcophagus of the fourth century, on a Brick Arch of the second, *taken with magnesian light.* 2096, 2097

In the centre of the sarcophagus, on a shield, are half-figures of the husband and wife interred in it. Around this sepulchral chamber is a podium, with small arched recesses, for the cinerary urns or vases (?)

[For the Paintings on these Tombs, see Catalogue of Fresco Paintings.]

Sarcophagus, now in the Colonna Garden. 2114

The small figure in the centre represents the defunct ; the group at the end is a subject from the amphitheatre ; a lion, stimulated by the *bestiarius* or keeper, devours a wild boar.

CHRISTIAN, OR MIXED SARCOPHAGI.

S. Helena, of red Porphyry, A.D. 330. 209

S. Constantia, of red Porphyry, A.D. 350, now in the Vatican Museum. 210

Shallow Sculpture of Vines and Cupids and Birds, now in the Porch of the Church of S. Lorenzo, f. m. 318

The Vintage. 2887

Allegorical subjects of the Vintage and Pasturage. (Cent. III.) 2917

Left side of the same. 2918

Lateran View of the Christian Museum. 2899

Genii, and over it a Cinerary Urn, with the Inscription, DIS MANIBUS . LU-CENA . T. L. STAPHYIA. 2254

Head of the defunct, and Jonah under the gourd, and at the angles Cupids and Psyches, or Genii. (Cent. IV.) 1327

CHRISTIAN SARCOPHAGI.

SARCOPHAGI WITH THE CREATION AND OTHER SCRIPTURAL SUBJECTS.

Lateran Museum—Sculpture—Sarcophagus of the fourth or fifth century, in the centre of which are the Busts of the two defuncts. 2902

In the upper part, on the left hand, is the Creation, and the representation of the Holy Trinity is very remarkable ; the Father behind the chair of the Son, and the Holy Ghost who, by laying on the hands, sanctifies the creatures,—Adam and Eve. On the right, the water turned to wine, the raising of Lazarus. In the lower part, the adoration of the Magi, Christ giving sight to the blind, Daniel in the lions' den, S. Peter and the sick, and other incidents.

View of the same (with two small Statues of the Good Shepherd, and fragments over them). 2903

Julia Juliana. The defunct is represented in the ark of Noah. 2938

Cover of the fourth century, representing two of the Apostles, and Lambs holding crowns in their mouths. 2910

Under it a sarcophagus representing the punishment of man, and some of the miracles of Christ.

CHRIST ordering the Apostles to feed His Lambs. 2924

CHRIST and ten Apostles, with two small figures of the donors kneeling at the feet of Christ, in the Crypt of Ancona Cathedral. (Cent. IV.) 2677

—— Figures in high-relief under arches, alternately round and triangular, in which Christ is represented in the centre, prophesying Peter's denial of Him before the Apostles. (Cent. IV.) 2909

CHRISTIAN SARCOPHAGI.

CHRIST AND THE APOSTLES. The Figures, beautifully carved in high relief, and placed under colonnades, with beautiful capitals, and the columns are enriched with spiral foliage. It is the finest panel of Christian sculpture that is known of that period. In this sarcophagus is represented the Ascension of Christ to Heaven. He gives a scroll to S. Peter, supposed to be conferring on him the legislative power.   2927

The Saviour and S. Peter with the Cock ; Miracles of the Saviour, and Buildings.   443, 444

     The two sides of the above sarcophagus. These are of quite a different style, in the shallow sculpture, usually some centuries later than this front, and were probably carved afterwards.

Two persons, of whom the Busts are sculptured in the central shell.   2900

     It represents various subjects in the life of Christ. The judgment of Pilate (the figure of Christ is omitted). Abraham sacrificing Isaac, and Moses receiving the Law. Under it Daniel in the lions' den ; the Prophets prophesying ; Christ and the Apostles preaching to the Jews. This sarcophagus is one of the finest works of Christian art.

VARIOUS SCRIPTURAL SUBJECTS.
(CENT. IV.)

Busts of the two defuncts.   2902

     In the upper part, on the left hand, is the Creation, and the representation of the Holy Trinity is very remarkable ; the Father behind the chair of the Son, and the Holy Ghost who, by laying on the hands, sanctifies the creatures,—Adam and Eve. On the right, the water turned to wine, the raising of Lazarus. In the lower part, the adoration of the Magi, Christ giving sight to the blind, Daniel in the lions' den, S. Peter and the sick, and other incidents.

History of Jonah, the Fishing, the Shepherd, the Resurrection of Lazarus, S. Peter striking the rock and taken prisoner, and Noah in the Ark. (Cent. V.)   2905

Subjects of the Old and New Testaments mixed together.   2907

     Adam and Eve, S. Peter with the Cock, Abraham and Isaac, &c.

Sacrifice of Abraham—Adam and Eve —and some miracles of Christ.   2912

     On the cover below it, Daniel—the Nativity—the adoration of the Magi —the multiplication of the Loaves— the preaching and imprisonment of S. Peter—a female figure reading the Gospel—and a slab with the name of CRISPINA.

Some of the Miracles of Christ, and an Orante.   2904

     This was found in the Catacomb of SS. Nereus and Achilleus.

Entrance of Christ into Jerusalem, the punishment of Man, and some of Christ's miracles.   2915

     On the cover under it, the Nativity, and the adoration of the Magi.

Monogram of Constantine—the imprisonment of S. Paul—Job—and the vocation of the people. Over it a Sculpture of the fourth century, representing a Supper, or Agape.   2929

Monogram, and the mysteries of the Passion. A small Sarcophagus, on which is represented the Codex of the Old and New Testaments, and a Supper.   2930

Fragment, representing S. Peter as Moses striking the rock, with two persons drinking at the stream (emblematic of his preaching) ; and the imprisonment of S. Peter.   2935

Miracles of Christ, the preaching and imprisonment of S. Peter.   2913

     On the cover below it, Jonah, Abraham, and Daniel.

Busts of the defuncts in the centre. 2914

     It represents Abraham symbolising the sacrifice of Christ ; while Peter, holding him by the arm, symbolises the Priesthood and the Sacrifice of the new law. In other parts, various miracles of Christ, and Moses receiving the Law. In the lower division, Peter and the Church, Daniel, the Marriage of Cana, &c.

A Cover, with some Miracles of Christ, and Daniel killing the Serpent. 2920

Under it a Sarcophagus with the busts of the defunct, and Bible subjects, among which the calling of Moses is very peculiar.

On a fragment of a cover, the offering of the Magi ; a side of a Sarcophagus with the departure of Elijah. 2932

Under it a funeral inscription, with the resurrection of Lazarus.

Sarcophagus of the fourth century, on the left of which is the preaching and imprisonment of S. Peter ; on the right, some miracles of Christ,—His entrance into Jerusalem. 2921

Sarcophagus for a youth, on which are represented the entrance of Christ into Jerusalem, the death of Pharaoh in the Red Sea, and other Scriptural subjects. 2933

—— Over this is another Sarcophagus with the genii of the seasons and tragic masks. Also a fragment of another representing a pastoral scene.

Sarcophagus with Christ before. Caiaphas, the denial of S. Peter, the Nativity, the baptism of Christ, and the resurrection of Lazarus. On the cover below, the three Jews in the burning fiery furnace, and a young man in the Ark instead of Noah. 2919

Miraculous events in the life of Christ, and His triumphal entrance into Jerusalem. 2906

Two Portraits of the defunct. 2911

The other subjects represented are all of the New Testament, excepting Daniel, Moses, Abraham, and Adam and Eve.

Christ prophesying Peter's denial of Him, and other subjects of the Bible ; the figures under small arches, round and triangular alternately, with fluted colonettes. 2916

—— some of the miracles of Christ, among which the Woman of Cana is peculiar ; the preaching and imprisonment of S. Peter. Below it are other fragments. 2922

Several Bible subjects—the resurrection of the Widow's son is represented in a peculiar manner. On the cover the history of Jonah—a youth in the Ark instead of Noah—the offering of the Magi—Moses receiving the Law—Adam and Eve. 2923

This cover, prepared for a Female, has afterwards been used for SABINVS, who lived forty-four years. 2925

The sarcophagus represents the usual Bible subjects ; in the centre is an Orante between two Apostles.

Three fragments of Sarcophagi. 2926

The Sarcophagus under them is ancient, but found recently, and badly restored.

Miracles of Christ, and three scenes in the life of S. Peter. 2931

Sacrifice of Abraham, and some miracles of Christ. 2934

CRYPT UNDER THE CHURCH OF S. PETER'S IN THE VATICAN. 231

The celebrated Sarcophagus of Junius Bassus, prefect of Rome, five times Consul, who died in the year 359 ; *taken with magnesian light.* 2997

The subjects represented in the upper part are :—

1. The Sacrifice of Abraham.
2. The Capture of S. Peter.
3. Christ seated between Peter and Paul.
4. The Capture of Christ.
5. Pilate washing his hands.

In the lower part are :—

1. Job on his mat, insulted by his Wife and his Friends.
2. Temptation of Adam and Eve.
3. Entrance of Christ into Jerusalem.
4. Daniel in the lions' den.
5. Capture of S. Paul.

Antique Sarcophagus used for the body of Pope Hadrian IV., A.D. 1169, the only English Pope (Breakspear) ; *taken with magnesian light.* 2992

[*The numbers refer to Mr. Parker's Catalogue.*]

CAPITALS.

IONIC, first century, a very fine one from the Lateran Museum, with Cornice. 1502, 2863

Ionic Capitals from the Villa of Lucius Verus, *c.* A.D. 150. 1493

CORINTHIAN, from the Villa of Lucius Verus, *c.* A.D. 150. 1497

Corinthian, from the Crypt of the Church of S. Cæcilia in Trastevere. 1864, 1865

COMPOSITE Capitals, with foliage of the Greek Acanthus, from the Lateran Museum, *c.* A.D. 120. 2859, 2861

Composite Capitals, from the Villa of Lucius Verus, *c.* A.D. 150. 1498, 1499

Composite Capital of Roman style, *c.* A.D. 200. 2865

Rich Composite Capital with figures, in the House of the Domitii, now the Villa Esmeade, *c.* A.D. 200. 2064

BASES AND BASEMENT MOULDINGS.

Basement and Mouldings of the Temple of Hercules, *c.* B.C. 10 (?) 1343

Base of a Column of the time of Augustus, A.D. 10, on the Palatine. 1347

Base and Fragment of a Column of the Basilica Ulpia. 739

Base, on the Palatine. 1348

Base of a Column in the Circus Alexandrinus. 94

Base of the fourth century. 2291

CORNICES.

Remains of Cornices of the Temples in the Forum Olitorium, of Spes and Juno Sospita. 1114, 1115

Cornice Mouldings of the lower story of the Colosseum, A.D. 80. 1346

Part of a Cornice, A.D. 75—100, in the Thermæ of Titus. 1881

Cornice of the Temple of Vespasian. 1670

Cornice of the Temple of Trajan. 815

Cornice of the Temple of Castor and Pollux in the Forum Romanum. 1684

Cornice, with foliage of the second century. 1503

Fragments of the Cornice of the Temple of the Sun (?), A.D. 274. 202

Fragment of a Cornice of the Temple of Mars (?), third century. 872

Cornice of the Arch of Constantine, A.D. 320. 1344

Capitals and Cornice of the Baptistery of S. John in fonte at the Lateran, *c.* A.D. 450. 387

CORNICE AND FRIEZE.

Cornice and Frieze of the Basilica Ulpia, *c.* A.D. 100, in the Forum of Trajan. 1494, 1495

Frieze of the Temple of Antoninus and Faustina, A.D. 138. 824

A Frieze of Sculptured foliage from the Basilica Ulpia, now in the Lateran Museum. 1493

Cornice and Capitals of the Temple of Castor and Pollux (?), in the Forum Romanum. 911

Cornice and Capitals of the Temple of Pallas, or Minerva, in the Forum Transitorium. 271

COLUMNS.

Columns of the Temple of Castor and Pollux in the Forum Romanum. 912

Antique Columns in the North Aisle of the Choir of the Church of S. Lorenzo. 594

Columns enriched with Shallow Sculpture of Ivy (Cent. IV.) (now in the Vatican Museum). 297

Columns of Peperino, of the Portico of the Temple of Hercules, the guardian of the Circus Flaminius, in the court of the Monastery of S. Nicola à Cesarini. 1642

Column of one of the three Temples, now in the Church of S. Nicolas in Carcere. 1112

Panels in the Thermæ of Titus, with elegant figures in bas-relief, first century, standing on fine antique bases. 1867, 1868, 1869

Door-post, with Shallow Carving of foliage and figures, second century, in the Lateran Museum. 2882

Cornice and Window in brickwork in part of the Pantheum of Agrippa, B.C. 26. 1237
Dio Cassius, l. liii. c. 27.

FRAGMENTS OF ARCHITECTURAL DETAILS.

Temples—Fragments of the ancient Temples in the Forum Olitorium. 1117

Fragments of Friezes, Capitals, &c. 2860, 2862, 2864, 2866, 2879, 2880

Fragments of the marble Ornaments of the Temple of the Arvales, c. A.D. 250. 1227

Fragments of Cornices in the Basilica Ulpia, in the Piazza di Colonna Trajana. 736

Broken Capital of the third century, found with the Marble Plan in 1867, at SS. Cosmas and Damian. 795

Capital of a Column of the Basilica Ulpia in the Piazza di Colonna Trajana. 740

Capitals of two Columns of the Portico of Octavia, near the Church of S. Angelo in Pescheria. 741

Capital from the Temple of Trajan. 813

Fragments of Cornice, &c., on the Platform now occupied by the Monastery of S. Francesca Romana. 825

Cornice and Tiles of the third century, found with the fragments of the Marble Plan in 1867, at SS. Cosmas and Damian. 798

Thermæ of Caracalla. Corinthian Capital and Column, found in 1868. 1069

Thermæ of Caracalla. Corinthian Capital, found in 1868. 1070

Gigantic Cornice, found at the Macao, near the Prætorian Camp. 2967

Base of a large Column of the third century. 2971
Found in the Forum Romanum, and now placed at the entrance to the Palaces of the Cæsars, with sculptures representing the three animals for sacrifice, the same as on the wall of the Comitium.

Fragments of Cornices and Bases of the second century, found in the Palazzo Fiano, in 1872, and now in the courtyard of the same palace. 2976, 2977, 2978, 2979

Cornices, &c., of the Temples of Spes, B.C. 261, and Pietas, B.C. 180, in the Forum Olitorium, now on the roof of the Church of S. Nicolas in Carcere. *From a Drawing.* 663, 666

MEDIEVAL ARCHITECTURAL DETAILS.
BRONZE DOORS.

Temples—Bronze Doors of the Pantheon. 771

Church of the Lateran—Ancient Bronze Door of the principal entrance. 937

Church of SS. Cosmas and Damian—Details of Doorway and Bronze Door of the Temple of Romulus, A.D. 320. 419

Lateran—Bronze Door, time of Celestin III., A.D. 1196, in the Baptistery of S. John in Fonte. 1713

Church of S. Antony the Abbot—Doorway, with Circular Head and Gothic Mouldings, c. A.D. 1200. 1088

Church of S. Alessio—Doorway ornamented with Ribbon Mosaics. 1916

Thirteenth Century—Church of S. John at Porta Latina — Square-headed Doorway with Mosaic ribbon of Cosmati work. 1176

Medieval—Doorway of the House of Stefano Porcaro in the Vicolo delle Ceste, No. 25 (A.D. 1316).   1333

Medieval—Gate of the old Hospital of the Lateran, A.D. 1446.   892

Medieval, Palazzo di Venezia—Doorway, A.D. 1480.   600

Sixteenth Century — Doorway in the Court of the Palazzo Gabrielli, *c.* A.D. 1500.   1402

Sixteenth Century — Doorway of the house called del Governo Vecchio, of the sixteenth century, with view into the court and arcade.   1401

Doorway of the sixteenth century in the Via del Gesù, No. 85, with good sculpture on the lintel.   1331

Sixteenth Century — Doorway of a House of the sixteenth century, in the Via dei Coronari, No. 45.   1396

Sixteenth Century—Door of the Astrologist, *c.* A.D. 1520 (?), near the Church of S. Eusebio.   961

WINDOWS.

Perforated Marble Window of the second century, now in the Crypt of the Church of Santi Quattro Coronati, on the Cœlian.   2090

Lateran, Cloister—Curious Window of pierced Marble (transenna) of the third century (?), with geometrical forms, and figure of S. John Evangelist.   1723

A Window or Loop-hole of the third century, in a Tomb near the Villa or Thermæ of the Gordiani.   877

Construction of a Window or Loop-hole of the third century, in the Thermæ of the Gordiani.   878

Construction of a Circular Window of the third century, in the Thermæ of the Gordiani, interior.   879

———— exterior.   880

Medieval Architecture—Window in the Belfry of S. Prassede, A.D. 820.   1504

A very curious early example of window-tracery, cut out of stucco.

Church of Ara Cœli — Window of Pierced Marble. Cent. XIV.   2275

Medieval House in the Ghetto—Ancient Window, *c.* A.D. 1400.   437

Medieval Iron Grille of Window, *c.* A.D. 1450, in a House in the Piazza di S. Egidio in Trastevere.   429

Medieval, Palazzo di Venezia—Window, A.D. 1480.   601

CHIMNEYS.

Chimney in the Monastery of S. Clement, twelfth century (?).   891

Modern Italian Chimneys.   846

CORNICES.

Cornice and curious Stucco Ornament of the ninth century (?), on the vault of the Crypt of S. Prassede.   1732

Sixteenth Century—Carved Cornice of a House in the Via dell' Anima, *c.* A.D. 1500.   1405

Churches — Prætorium of S. Stefano Rotondo. Details. The Ionic Capitals, A.D. 467; the Corinthian, A.D. 632 (?), when it was made into a Church.   214

Capitals, two Antique, one Medieval imitation, in the Church of S. Maria in Cosmedin.   637

Basilica of Constantine — Details of Terra Cotta Vault, A.D. 330.   205

CHRISTIAN SCULPTURE IN CHURCHES.

[*The numbers refer to Mr. Parker's Catalogue.*]

STATUES.

OF THE PROPHETS.

Lateran Museum—Statue of the fourth century, smaller than life, representing the Good Shepherd, with a Lamb on His shoulder. Cent. IV.   **2901**

The celebrated Moses of Michael Angelo in the Church of S. Pietro in Vincoli. Cent. XVII.   **1932**

Statue of the Prophet Elias, by Lorenzetti, in the Church of S. Maria del Popolo. Cent. XVII.   **2282**

Statue of Jonah, from a drawing of Raphael, in the Church of S. Maria del Popolo. Cent. XVII.   **2281**
Some say that it was also carved by Raphael.

OF THE SAINTS, &c.

Bronze Figure of S. John Baptist, by G. B. della Porta, in the Baptistery of S. John in Fonte, near the Lateran. Cent. XVII.   **1712**

Crypt of S. Peter — The celebrated Statue of S. Peter, formerly under the portico of the old Basilica. Cent. II. and XVI. *Taken with magnesian light.*   **2995**
The Apostle is represented seated, holding the keys. The figure, which recalls the statues of the Consuls, is antique; the head is of the sixteenth century, and the hands are modern.

Bronze Figures of S. Lucius, Pope, S. Urban, Pope, and S. Maximus, Martyr, A.D. 1600, in the Church of S. Cecilia in Trastevere.   **1708**

Bronze Figures of three Saints, S. Valerian, S. Cecilia, and S. Tiburtius, in the Church of S. Cecilia in Trastevere, A.D. 1600.   **1707**

The celebrated Figure of S. Cecilia by Stefano Maderno, from the Church in the Trastevere dedicated in her name. Cent. XVII.   **1705**
The body of the Saint is represented by the sculptor as it was found when her tomb was opened.

OUT OF ROME.

Ancona — Cathedral — Curious small figure of a Bishop standing with his crozier and mitre, in the crypt. Cent. XIII.   **2674**

Loreto—Bronze Statue of Sixtus V., seated. Cent. XVI.   **2682**

BAS-RELIEFS,

VARIOUS SUBJECTS.

FROM THE CRYPT OF S. PETER'S.

Taken with magnesian light.

Bas-relief from the Ciborium of Pius II., A.D. 1460. Two angels holding the head of S. Andrew.   **2996**

Sculpture from the Tomb of Cardinal Berardus Herulus, of Narni, A.D. 1479.   **2990**
It represents the Almighty in the act of blessing, holding a book, and surrounded by Angels with eight wings.

Ciborium of the Holy Lance (time of Innocent VIII., A.D. 1490), two Angels adoring the Holy Relic.   **2989**

F

Sculpture in white marble representing S. John the Evangelist.   2991

This sculpture was ordered by Innocent VIII., A.D. 1490, to decorate the Ciborium of the Holy Lance, with the other three Evangelists.

A Bas-relief made at the end of the sixteenth century, under Pope Sixtus V.   2993

This splendid bas-relief was made to decorate the front of the Altar of the Pope. It represents the Judgment of the Apostles by Nero.

(For two Sarcophagi in the Crypt of S. Peter, see Sarcophagi.)

FROM THE LATERAN, &c.

Lateran, Cloister—Figure of S. John Evangelist.   1723

Church of S. Pietro in Vincoli—Bas-relief representing S. Peter with the Keys and Chains, A.D. 1465.   1930

On his right hand the Cardinal donor kneeling, on his left an Angel holding the chain.

Lateran Museum—Sculpture—Bas-relief, representing the three Jews in the burning fiery furnace, and Noah in the Ark. Cent. IV. (?)   2908

Under it several fragments.

Church of S. Pudentiana—Doorway as restored in 1872. Cent. VIII. (?)   3060

The columns and the shallow sculpture of the heads are ancient, representing the family of Pudens.

—— The same, before the restoration.   279

—— Sculpture, in the Gaetani Chapel, behind the altar.   3061

The offering of the Magi in fine alto-relievo, c. A.D. 1600.

OUT OF ROME.

SUBIACO.

Curious Medieval Bas-relief, and Inscription of the Dedication of the Church of S. Scholastica. Cent. X. (?)   1567

DEDICATA EST AN AB INCARNA-

TIONE DOMINI CCCCCCCCCLXXXI M. DECB DIIII INDICTIONE VIII.

A wolf and a stag are represented drinking out of the same cup or calyx.

LUCCA.

Bas-relief with Inscription, under the Portico of the Duomo. Cent. XII. Representing the legend of S. Martin, with allegorical figures of six of the months under arches in panels.   3068

Bas-relief with Inscription, over the principal Door of the Duomo. Cent. XII.   3069

It represents S. Maria and the twelve Apostles, with their names under each, in sculpture of the thirteenth century. In the tympanum above is the ascension of Christ in an aureole, supported by two angels.

Church called the "Oratory," curious Bas-relief over the Door.   3080

This is a very curious and early piece of sculpture of about the middle of the twelfth century, apparently representing the legend of S. John Evangelist. In the centre is the saint in the cauldron of boiling oil ; on either side is a small temple, with a domical vault, and shafts having twisted fluting round them. It may probably be the work of the same sculptor as the celebrated font in S. Frediano, who has there inscribed his name and date, Robertus, 1151.

Church of S. John. Principal Door, with fine Sculpture. Cent. XII. 3075

ANCONA.

Cathedral—Panel of Sculpture of the thirteenth century, in the crypt. 2675

Christ and two of the emblems of the evangelist with vines. Under it is the inscription :—

MAGISTER . FILIP . ME FECIT.

—— Panel of Sculpture of the Madonna, with the infant Christ and two saints, in the Crypt. Cent. XIV. (?)   2678

Benevento—Church of S. Sofia—West Door, with a group of Sculpture in the Tympanum. Cent. XIII. 2687

HOUSE OF THE BLESSED VIRGIN AT LORETO.

The figures of Prophets, A.D. 1520.
1107
The Annunciation, A.D. 1520. 1105
The Nativity over a Doorway, with the Arms of the Medici, Leo X., A.D. 1520. 1103
The Presentation in the Temple, A.D. 1520. 1104
The Santissima Casa carried by Angels, A.D. 1520. 1106, 2680
Cathedral at Arezzo—Sculpture behind the Altar. Cent. XIII. (?) 521

BAS-RELIEFS ON BRONZE AND WOODEN DOORS, IN CHURCHES.

Bas-relief of the seventeenth century, carved on the wooden door of the Church of S. Sabina. 1647
Representing several subjects from the Bible.
Church of S. Pietro in Vincoli—Bronze Door, by Vignola, with panel of bas-relief. Cent. XVII. (?) 1933

OUT OF ROME.

PISA—Details of Bronze Doors of the Cathedral. Cent. XII. (?) 501
Benevento—Cathedral—Rich Bronze Doors at the west end, (Cent. XII.), said to have been made at Constantinople. 2684

DOORWAYS, &c., WITH SCULPTURE, IN CHURCHES.

Crypt of S. Peter—A fine Door-post of Marble, used in the Chapel of John VII., A.D. 706, with animals, birds, foliage, and figures. *Taken with magnesian light.* 2985, 2986, 2987
Sculptured Doorway of the Church of S. Stephen in the Leonine City, or Borgo (S. Stefano dei Mori), c. A.D. 1200. 269

Church of S. Maria in Trastevere—Doorway, with fine Sculpture, built by Cardinal Marcus Syticus, A.D. 1625. 1905, 1906

DOORWAYS, OUT OF ROME.

Lucca — Church of S. Christopher. Principal Door, with fine mouldings and capitals. Cent. XII. 3073
—— Church of S. Giusto. Cent. XII. Front view, shewing Sculptured Doorway. 3077
Subiaco—Gothic Archway in the Cloister of S. Scholastica, A.D. 1235, with figure of the Madonna. 1566
Naples—Door and Sculptured Doorway of the Church of S. Gennaro. Cent. XV. 2134
Vico-Varo—View of the Church called the "Tempietto," shewing the Sculptured Doorway. Cent. XVI. (?) 3046
Pisa—Door of Baptistery, with Sculptures. Cent. XIII. (?) 504

VARIOUS OBJECTS FROM CHURCHES, WITH SHALLOW SCULPTURE.

Marble Seat of S. Gregory in the Church of S. Stefano Rotondo, c. A.D. 590. 359
Marble Table at which S. Gregory fed the poor, c. A.D. 590. 217
Well in Marble in the garden, near the Church of S. John at the Porta Latina, c. A.D. 750. 263, 569
Cloister of the Lateran, c. A.D. 1300. Well with Shallow Sculpture, c. A.D. 850. 1077
Church of S. M. de Priorato, on the Aventine—Marble Coffer, or Reliquary, c. A.D. 750 (?). 314
Church of S. Maria in Trastevere—Portions of a Screen with Shallow Sculpture, c. A.D. 800, built into the wall of the Porch in the time of Clement XI., A.D. 1700—1721. 1907, 1908, 1909
Paschal Candlestick in the Church of S. Paul f. m. Cent. XIII. (?) 2018
Lions at the Door of the Church of S. Lorenzo, f. m. c. A.D. 1220. 317

Lateran, Cloister—Lions at the door, &c. Cent. XIII. (?)   1720

The "Bocca.de la Verita" in the Porch of the Church of S. Maria in Cosmedin. Cent. III. (?)   636

IVORY CARVINGS.

Ivory Pixis of the eighth century (?), (now in the possession of Alexander Nisbet, Esq.) It was found in Rome, and probably came from the Church of S. Mennas, which was near S. Paul's f. m., representing the Legend of S. Mennas, an Egyptian Martyr, A.D. 304, (vide Surius).

1780, 1781, 1782, 1783

CURIOUS INCISED SLABS.

ANCONA—Figures of Saints on early incised slabs, in the crypt of the Cathedral. Cent. XIV. (?) 2672, 2676

Catacombs—S. Nereo. Figure of the Good Shepherd, and a dove with the olive-branch, the emblem of peace, incised on a tombstone, c. A.D. 320. *Taken with magnesian light.*   1617

For other incised figures and emblems, see Inscriptions in the Lateran, &c.

For additional Christian Sculptures see Medieval Tombs, &c., in the Churches, Nos. 316, 320, 650, 651, 1392, 1398, 1484, 1646, 1701, 1702, 1703, 1721, 1724, 1910, 1911, 1929, 2073, 2267, 2268, 2269, 2278, 2280, 2673.

See also Monsignor de Montault's Photographs of Christian Sarcophagi, &c., in the Ashmolean Museum.

www.ingramcontent.com/pod-product-compliance
Lightning Source LLC
Chambersburg PA
CBHW020750020726
47495CB00008B/2358